RICH BITCH

THE MEANEST
OF THEM ALL

A NOVEL BY
TIFFANI MURPHY

PUBLISHER'S NOTE:
This book is a work of fiction. Names, characters, businesses,
Organizations, places, events and incidents are the product of the
Author's imagination or are used fictionally. Any resemblance of
Actual persons, living or dead, events, or locales are entirely coin-
cidental.

Library of Congress Control Number: 2014911825

ISBN 10: 0989790150

ISBN 13: 978-0989790154

Cover Design: Davida Baldwin www.oddballdsgn.com
Editor(s): T. Styles; C. Washington & S. Ward
www.richbitchpublications.com
First Edition

Printed in the United States of America

ACKNOWLEDGEMENTS

I'ma keep this short and sweet, like my circle. To my family thank you for always being there to support me no matter what. To my sister Chanel thanks for helping me see the dream and bringing it to light. Your book The Pussy Mob was bananas. Can't wait to see what else you do when you back on the block. I love you. To all the readers, thanks for choosing my novel and I hope you like my flavor.

Tiffani Murphy
The Meanest of Them All
www.richbitchpublications.com

DEDICATION

I dedicate this book to all my Rich Bitches. Get money.

CHAPTER ONE
JANUARY 20, 2014

Dear Diary,
Today I don't feel like writing. But mama told me to always record time. That even the prettiest girls can forget the good stuff and that my diary will remind me to count my blessings.

I forgot to ask mama what to do when you have nothing to be grateful for. But now it's too late.

Saturday, March 2nd 2013

The air from the vent caressed Morgan's eyelids as her cheek pressed against the cool glass. Her face was puffy due to crying so much and her hands were clasped together in her lap. As she watched the landmarks pass by she tried to conceal the hate in her heart for her parents.

"Do you feel like you're older now?" Annie asked placing her hand on her daughter's thigh.

Silence.

"Because you don't look a day over thirteen."

Morgan sighed in irritation. She knew her mother was trying to make her laugh but at the moment she hated her. She could smell the bananas stemming from the bags of groceries that sat on the backseat. After she learned that she wasn't getting a car, Annie made her go with her to the grocery store.

"I never get what I want," Morgan finally said. "It's all about the sisters but never about me. You and daddy don't treat me the same." She could still remember when she was the only one in the home, before her sisters were born, even though it was brief. Those were the good old days. Annie and Hollis would buy her anything she desired and nothing seemed to be off limits. But now that her sisters were there, it felt like she was always the last one they needed to worry about and it enraged her and made her resent her sisters even more.

Annie looked over at her when she reached a red light. "You know that's not true."

"It is," she persisted with pouted lips. Morgan sat up straight and gazed at the rain that suddenly started slapping against the car and windshield. "Why won't he let me get a car? I never ask for anything and you promised to at least think about it."

Annie focused on the road. "You heard your father, honey. It's dangerous."

"But I know there is another reason. Why won't you tell me?"

Annie sighed. "Because I almost died in one." Her voice was low as she admitted a secret. "It was right before I married your father." She paused. "During one of my mental breaks." She looked ahead and tried to push away the embarrassment. "I was driving up a road and my mind wandered. I thought the lines on the road had curved suddenly and I followed them. Turns out it was all in my head. When I followed the new pattern though, it led me toward the railing of a bridge. I would've gone over had the railing not been steady and made of iron." She looked over at her daughter briefly. "That's why you or he have to always go with me when I drive. And that's why he doesn't want you to drive, Morgan. It's not because he doesn't want you to be happy, or me. He loves you but we don't know if you girls are suffering from this illness even though all of you aren't showing signs."

"I'm not the one who's crazy," Morgan admitted. "Petra is." Morgan's body stiffened. It was a known fact that Annie suffered from a mental disorder and Morgan worried that her sisters Shaye and Petra, who were also different, suffered from the same thing. But in her mind she was fine and would never be like them, or her mother. But Morgan wasn't blind either and she knew there was a possibility that Annie was right.

There were many nights in the Collins home when Annie would rant and rave. She would even go off on her children during these times if they got in her way. In fact, one day Morgan was home alone with her mother while the rest of the family made a midnight run for ice cream to a local 7-Eleven.

Annie was in the kitchen fussing to herself that she wouldn't let anybody take her away from her family. Morgan approached her in an effort to soothe her, although Hollis warned her to never do that. The rule was that when Annie 'Got Into the Collins Way', she should go to her room and lock the door. But Morgan disobeyed the order and approached Annie while she was cooking a pan with nothing inside of it on the stove.

When Morgan touched her arm Annie flung around with the pan and burned her daughter's wrist. Morgan was horrified and stumbled backwards to save herself. But Annie, believing her daughter was the CIA, lit a hand towel and ran after Morgan to set her body on fire. Luckily, Morgan was able to get in her bedroom just in time to save herself before Hollis came home a minute later and was able to get Annie under control. But the event never left Morgan's mind or heart, which was why she couldn't stand fire at all. She still had the burn mark on her wrist as a reminder.

If Annie wasn't ranting, she would sleepwalk in the middle of the night, only for them to find her in the dark streets, roaming. One time they found her at 4:00 in the morning with her clothing soiled in blood. Nine months later, Shaye was born. Although Shaye looked nothing like the rest of the Collins family, with the exception of Annie that is, Hollis still treated her as his child. But, there was a great possibility that Shaye was a product of rape, and Hollis and Annie kept the secret to themselves, even away from their daughters.

"Is that why you let Petra get away with so much? Because she's like you?"

Annie exhaled and continued up the road although the rain was coming down harder. "I know Petra and Shaye aren't like the rest of you. And it doesn't mean they're ignorant or dumb because I don't believe I am. It's just that they have to manage their illness, Morgan. With a little prayer and love, they'll be fine. But you have to stick together. You have to be there for one another. And since you are the oldest, I'm counting on you."

"But I don't want to be in charge of anything or anybody, mama. I just wanna be me and hang out with my friends."

"But you might not have a choice, baby."

The sky grew darker and water slammed harder against the car, causing it to sway a little. Suddenly large spears of lightning flashed everywhere. Morgan's muscles tensed up as she witnessed the violent display in the sky.

"Wow, they said it would rain but I didn't know it would be this bad," Annie said.

"I want to go home," Morgan responded. "Trevor said he couldn't stay that long anyway. I wanna get back before he leaves." The weather was frightening her, which was the real reason for her mood.

Annie looked over at her again and touched her leg. "Okay, honey." She paused. "Remember what I said about—"

A large tree slammed on the left side of the car, sending the vehicle flying in the air. When it landed back on the ground it flew against a light pole that crashed onto the hood and on top of Annie's body.

Morgan could suddenly smell the odor of gas and when she glanced over at her mother, she saw she was moaning and appeared to be in a lot of pain. Morgan was sore too but it wasn't as bad.

"Mama," Morgan said as blood from an open wound on the top of her head trailed down her face and over her eyes. "Are you okay?"

Annie didn't respond. Her face scrunched up and she continued to groan. When Morgan leaned up and looked closer at her mother she gasped. The left side of Annie's face was scraped away, revealing the socket of her eye and the bone underneath.

"Oh, my God. Mama! Your face!" Morgan's body trembled because she'd never seen anything so horrible. She popped the seatbelt off and leaned closer to her mother. The odor of gasoline was so strong she was certain that it was on her clothing. "Can you move, mama? Because we have to get out of the car. It's going to blow up." When she tried to reach over her to release the seatbelt Annie screamed out in agony. It was difficult to get to her body because of the pole that was pushing against her head.

"Don't do it like that, Morgan!" she yelled. "Get out of the car and try to help me from the driver's side."

Morgan jumped back and her body pressed against the dented door and she placed her hand over her mouth. In all of her life, her mother never spoke to her so harshly, unless she was ranting. Was she losing her mind now?

When Annie glanced at Morgan with most of her facial features gone she saw that her child was frightened. "I'm sorry, baby," she said as she inhaled rapidly to grab some air. "Don't be afraid. I'll be fine," she said before gasping. She was trying her best to remain calm but she ached in every place imaginable. "But w-what I need you to do right now is get out of the car and open my door. Okay? But be careful."

"Mama, I'm scared."

"I know, baby," she smiled. "But I need your help because I can't move myself." She paused. "Get out and open my car door to help me. Do it now or the car may blow. We don't have a lot of time."

The rain was coming down so hard it was difficult for Morgan to hear her mother speak. But having gotten the gist of what she wanted done,

Morgan pulled the latch to the door. It opened and she rolled out and fell to the ground.

It wasn't until her hands and knees slammed against the concrete that she realized a branch had pierced her wrist. It entered one side of her flesh and stuck out from the other. At the moment so much adrenaline coursed through her veins that she couldn't feel the pain.

Instead she hopped up, and hobbled toward the left side of the car as her mother requested. Once there, she pulled the driver's side door, which was dented, but it wouldn't give. Morgan tugged several more times but it still refused to open.

"Mama, it's not working," she yelled. She could now see that the entire left side of her face was missing and she resembled a monster. "I don't know what to do!"

"Just keep trying, baby," Annie moaned. "I'm counting on you."

Morgan obeyed her mother and when she pulled the handle again slightly harder, a large flame exploded from the hood of the car. The burst was so huge that it singed the front part of Morgan's hair before settling down and staying on the vehicle.

Seeing the large orange blaze, Morgan's rear slapped against the ground and she scooted back away from the car. The blaze hadn't reached Annie yet but it was on the way. Luckily, the door that once blocked Morgan's path from her mother had blown off because of the explosion and was lying on the ground. All Morgan had to do was pull her out and she would be saved.

"Baby, help me," Annie said with an extended hand. "Pull me out." She was immobile due to the seatbelt being strapped to her body. And due to the crash, she was paralyzed from the waist down.

"I'm scared, mama," she pleaded. Tears rolled down Morgan's face along with the rain as she shook her head softly from left to right. She was too afraid of the fire. Too afraid of burning and too afraid of conquering her fear.

"Baby, please," Annie pleaded, as the fire moved dangerously close to the front of her body. "I need your help. I can't get out by myself. I can't move. Without you, I will die."

CHAPTER TWO
2 WEEKS LATER

The happy life as Morgan Collins knew it was over.

Annie Collins died on Morgan's birthday and she was devastated.

Water ran cold over Morgan's hands in the sink as she washed a frying pan that was already clean. A damp baby blue hand towel rested on her shoulder, the same one Annie always carried, as thoughts of losing her passed through her mind. The entire family mourned Annie's loss but none as greatly as Morgan.

She was there.

She witnessed firsthand the accident and due to fear, she watched her mother take her last breath. The picture would remain etched in her mind forever. It was because of her that she was dead and she would never forgive herself.

Morgan continued at her chore until she placed the last glass in the dish rack on the counter. She would've used the dishwasher instead but it was filled to capacity, mainly because every other day someone was over the house to give the Collins family their condolences, even though they didn't want them. What they wanted was to be left alone.

When Morgan finished she turned around, leaned up against the counter and looked at her sisters who were sitting around the table. First she considered Petra. Her curly, wild hair was dry and brittle due to her not caring for it since Annie was gone. The right side of her face was resting on the table and she was looking directly at Morgan with suspicious eyes.

Petra was always good with picking up on things that others chose to ignore and now she was wondering if Morgan had anything to do with their mother's death. After all, she was angry earlier that day when she learned she wasn't getting the car. What was to stop her from taking her life?

Feeling Petra's scrutinizing glare, Morgan's eyes focused on 14-year-old Lexia next. A red bowl set on the table beside her, which was filled with melted vanilla ice cream that she wanted at first but now couldn't stomach. Her long messy braids sat in a wild bun on top of her head and one of them dipped into the bowl. Out of everyone in the family, Lexia was the most adventurous. If she wasn't skateboarding with her friends, that earned her five broken bones, she was climbing the large oak tree in the back of the house which Hollis and Annie forbade her to climb.

Across from Lexia sat 13-year-old Grace with her arms folded on her chest and a grumpy look on her face. A Band-Aid was stuck to the skin under her right eye and her hair, which usually rocked a bob, was pulled back into a short ponytail.

There was no denying that when it came to a good fight, Grace was the girl to go to in the Collins family. She didn't back down from anything or anyone, and that included the teachers at her school, which was why she was always in trouble. Although she could wreck with the hands, she suffered from the superhero syndrome. She believed in fighting for those who couldn't fight for themselves.

11-year-old Shaye, the quietest of them all, slouched over in her seat as she played with her fingers. Every so often, she would scratch at her hair, which was cut into a short-cropped boy hairstyle, to prevent her from pulling it from her scalp. Although she didn't speak, she could cook, having watched Annie closely every day of her life. And Shaye enjoyed making food for her family too.

Morgan's head hung low and she tossed the hand towel on the sink. Her family was destroyed and she felt responsible. It was up to her to help them get back together. But how could she bring her family back? She was a child herself.

She raked her hair backwards with her fingers, pushed off of the counter and addressed her sisters. "Mama is gone," she said softly, her voice almost unrecognizable. "I know it doesn't feel good but it's true." She could feel herself about to choke up but she held it together. Although it was obvious that Annie was gone since they recently attended the funeral, they hadn't spoken of it until that moment. "We are all going to miss her but we have to be strong. She would want it that way."

"How the fuck you know what mama wants?" Petra yelled as she lifted her head from the table. "You not her and you won't ever be so don't start trying to act like it either."

"I don't want to be mama," she responded. "I just want us to stick together because we're going to need each other more."

"But how?" Grace asked through clenched teeth. "Kids not supposed to be without they mother. So why we ain't got one no more?"

"She's right," Lexia added. "Stuff ain't been right around here since she died. Shaye pissing in the bed more and Petra done burnt two trees down to the ground a few blocks over." She looked at her with lowered eyes. "Even though she think nobody know."

"It wasn't me!" Petra yelled as she slammed her fist on top of the table. It rocked a little and startled the others. "That's why I hate ya'll. You always taking everybody else's side but mine!"

When Petra and Grace took to screaming at each other, Morgan grabbed a cast iron pan off the dish rack and tossed it on the table. It spun around a few times before stopping. The ringing noise scared the sisters into silence.

When they were quiet Morgan moved closer to them. "We can't be fighting each other. No more anyway. Mama wouldn't want us to be in here going at each other's throats. You know she always wanted us to be close. Outside of daddy, we all we got." She looked at her sisters to check for understanding. "You're right, Grace. Kids not supposed to be without they mother but we don't have a choice. She's gone."

"How you get away?" Petra asked through clenched teeth.

"What you talking about?"

"You know, bitch. How mama gone but you alive when ya'll were together. How did that happen?"

Morgan's heartbeat kicked around in her chest and she moved uneasily in place. "I told you." She swallowed. "I got out just before the fire blew the car up. There was nothing I could do."

"Stop it, Petra," Grace said.

"No. I won't stop it!" Petra stood up and scratched her wild curly hair. She stepped closer to Morgan with squinted eyes. "Like I was saying, it's mighty funny that mama was burned to dust and all you got was that hole in your wrist." She pointed at her arm. "I don't know what happened to mama but I do know you ain't help like you claimed. And I hate you for it!" She rolled her eyes and stormed up the steps. "And nobody putting me back in no home either! I'm not going!"

Morgan knew her sister was right and the guilt was overwhelming. She averted her eyes from the others and turned around to face the sink. The back of her neck started sweating and her chin quivered as she tried desperately not to cry out loud.

Grace walked up to Morgan and stood at her side. When she saw tears filling up in the wells of Morgan's eyes she grabbed a paper towel and wiped them away. "I don't know what it must've been like for you."

"What do you mean?" Morgan sniffled.

"To see mama killed and all." She paused. "But I do know that you did all you could to save her so don't listen to Petra. She just hurt."

"It is my f-fault," she stuttered.

"Don't say that. And don't worry about Petra either. She'll come around, Morgan. Wait, you'll see."

Hearing how kind her sister was to her even though she knew she didn't deserve it caused her to cry harder.

When she felt someone gripping one of her legs she looked down and saw Shaye. Shaye didn't speak much but she expressed herself in other ways and the Collins sisters understood her when the world did not.

"She just mad mama is gone," Grace continued. "We all are. But we gonna be fine."

"Yeah, and we don't blame you either," Lexia added, her face red from sobbing all day. "Just give Petra some time."

Morgan wiped the tears away. She never told anyone how she left her mother for dead because she was too afraid of the fire. Besides, she couldn't bear to lose them too.

"Thank you," she said hugging them. "Thank you, sisters." She wiped the tears with the back of her hand and exhaled. "Because I really did everything I could."

Lexia sighed. "I know and I miss her already." She paused. "But somebody gotta go upstairs to talk to daddy," she said. "He hasn't come out of his room since the funeral."

"I know. I went upstairs earlier today to give him something to eat but he just shook his head and said to put it on the dresser. He said he don't want to do nothing but lay in his room and d—"

"Don't say it," Morgan stopped her. "I'll go talk to him."

She pulled away from her sisters and moved slowly up the stairs. Although her mother had been gone for weeks, she could still smell the scent of her favorite perfume in the hallways and it made her stomach churn.

When she got to her parents' door she opened it without knocking. Annie and Hollis always said that if the door was unlocked the girls could come in so she didn't knock. When the door opened a stale odor filled the air. Hollis was sitting on the edge of his bed looking out of the window with his back faced in Morgan's direction. A cloud of smoke hovered over his head like a heavy fog.

THE MEANEST OF THEM ALL

"You girls okay down there?" he asked without looking.

"Yeah." She paused and swallowed. "Kinda."

"What's wrong?"

"Nothing, just worried about you and wondering why you not eating." She took two more steps in his direction but stopped before reaching him. "Daddy," she whispered, "how come you won't eat? Shaye and Grace said they keep bringing plates up here but you send them back. Are you okay?"

"What do you mean, Morgan?"

"I don't think you're supposed to go that long without eating. Can I pour you some water at least?"

"I'll eat later on today. Try not to worry. Okay?" He smashed the cigarette out on the edge of the wooden headboard.

"Can I talk to you about something?" Morgan walked deeper into the room and bypassed the dresser. On top of it were old plates of food, some of which were molded.

"You know you never have to ask me that. What's on your mind?"

"Are you mad at me?" she stood directly in front of him, partially blocking his view of the window in the process. "For what happened to mama?"

Hollis looked around her out of the window. "What's happening to our family is not your fault, Morgan. A man has to grieve and this is my way of doing it. That's all. Try not to blame yourself." His voice was cold and rattled her.

Hoping to soften him up she dropped to her knees and looked up at him. His light skin was ashy where the tears had run down his cheeks and dried. She placed her head on his thigh and waited for him to rub her hair like he did whenever she was sad. Instead, he remained cold and she smelled a strong odor of cigarettes mixed with dried urine since he hadn't washed in weeks. "I hate that you're hurting, daddy." Tears released themselves from her eyes and dampened his jeans. "Can I do anything for you?"

Finally, he rubbed her hair and she was relieved. Maybe her daddy was coming back. "No, baby girl. I'm going to be okay. But with your mother gone you are the woman of the house now and I'm going to need you to keep your sisters straight. They listen to you. Can you do that for me?"

"Of course, daddy. I'd do anything."

"I'm devastated," he said as he rubbed his red hair backwards. "I just lost the only woman I loved for more than thirty years. But I have to get it together for our family, for you girls. I just need a little time."

Morgan stood on her knees and looked into her father's eyes. In all of her young years, she'd never seen him so distraught. She wanted him to be happy again. She wanted him to play ball with them out front. Take them to the movies and enjoy picnics with them at the park. He was such a good father that she was willing to do whatever she could to take care of the family, including satisfying her father's every need.

"I can take care of us, daddy." She wiggled herself between his legs and placed her hands on his thighs. "I'm bigger now. I'll be eighteen next year and everything."

He smiled at her and ran his hand down the side of her face. "I know you can, baby girl."

Morgan smiled and leaned her body toward him. He grinned and lowered his head so that their lips met. The kiss seemed innocent enough until Morgan snaked her tongue between her father's rough lips and inside of his warm menthol flavored mouth.

Hollis was confused at first, not knowing what was happening. But when he opened his eyes and saw that his daughter's lids were shut he knew exactly what was going on.

He quickly separated his lips from hers, placed his hands on her shoulders and softly pushed her backwards. "Morgan, not like this." He couldn't believe his baby girl just kissed him in such a passionate way and he immediately felt like he was to blame. Maybe he gave her the wrong impression and he would never forgive himself.

Morgan wasn't feeling any better. Embarrassed by her actions and that she was rejected; she was on the verge of crying. But Hollis smiled and said, "This isn't your fault. It's mine." He stood up and helped Morgan to her feet. Without another word, he walked her to the door, led her out and smiled at her. "I love you, baby girl. And I'll make this right. I know just what to do." He softly closed the door.

Instead of leaving, Morgan stood at the door for another five minutes as she battled with whether to go in and apologize or not. After an hour she realized she needed to give him his space. Besides, she was too embarrassed to say anything else to him at the moment anyway.

Slowly she trudged to her room. She grabbed the diary under the bed and wrote her most precious secrets inside of the pages. It took her five hours to get some sleep and she felt so bad she contemplated running away from home. Would he look at her differently? Maybe leaving was best. But how could she leave when her sisters needed her? Her father was right. She was the oldest and it was time to stop being selfish and take care of her family.

When Morgan woke up the next morning she could smell bacon cooking. When she walked downstairs she was not surprised that Shaye, although young, prepared breakfast for everyone. Although the untraditional meal included vanilla cupcakes, which were Morgan's favorite and bacon and eggs, the meal did hit the spot.

After dinner that night, Morgan's sisters sat in front of the TV and watched reruns of their favorite reality shows. But Morgan's eyes remained glued to her father's door. Was he in the house? His car was still out front but it wasn't uncommon for a friend to pick him up from time to time or for him to walk a few blocks down the street and catch a cab. So she couldn't be sure if he was home or not.

No one heard from Hollis the entire day and although her sisters went to their rooms and to bed, she stayed in the living room. She couldn't bear not speaking to her father and decided to apologize for trying to kiss him.

When she finally heard keys turning the locks it was midnight. Morgan rubbed her eyes, planted her feet on the floor and walked toward the front door. When it opened she saw her father, who smiled so brightly at her she knew their troubles were over.

"Oh, daddy, I missed you so much," she said wrapping her arms around his waist. "I was worried."

"I missed you too, baby."

When she separated from him and took two steps back she saw a woman was standing in the doorway behind him.

"Honey, I want to introduce you to your new stepmother." He rubbed Morgan's hair softly backwards. "Her name is Lisa."

THE MEANEST OF THEM ALL

CHAPTER THREE
MARCH 18TH, 2013

Dear Diary,
Today I feel bad. I tried to kiss daddy and I hope mama didn't see me up in heaven. I wasn't being nasty. I just wanted to stop him from being so sad. Since it's my fault mama ain't here anyway.
Now he got a new wife.
I pray I like her.
I pray she likes me.

March 19, 2013

Something bad was coming and Morgan could tell by the change in the weather. At first the sky was clear and the sun shined brightly on the sisters as they walked home from school with Trevor,

Morgan's boyfriend. But now, large grey clouds covered the edges of the sun, darkening the sky in the process.

"We gotta hurry up home," Morgan said to Grace and Lexia as she surveyed the sky. They were walking ahead of Morgan and Trevor and were in a deep conversation about the new step-mother when their sister interrupted. "It's gonna rain soon and I don't want to be here when it happens." Every time it rained, flashbacks of losing her mother ravaged her mind.

Grace and Lexia looked back at Morgan with irritation painted on their faces. "We moving as fast as we can," Lexia said as she rolled her eyes. "Stop rushing us." Although they were annoyed, they picked up the pace. The last thing they needed was to get smacked in front of Trevor, since all of the Collins sisters had crushes on him.

Morgan adjusted the large blue book bag that weighed down her shoulder and Trevor gripped her hand as he rubbed his thumb in the center of her palm. When her stomach fluttered, she knew what he wanted. Sex. There was never a day that went by where he didn't tell her. So she slid her hand away. "Thank you for walking me home," she said as she looked up at him to judge his mood. "I know you don't have to do it."

Trevor, a seventeen-year-old quarterback at Morgan's high school, was stunning. At 6'2" with dark chocolate skin and a sculpted physique, he would drive anyone crazy, especially a teenage girl.

He shrugged and his lips tightened. "Not a problem." He paused. "So you think she's gonna be a good fit?" He stuffed his hands in his pockets to avoid touching her. Even though Morgan was a virgin, she still turned him on. "Your stepmother?"

"I don't know," she whispered. "We never seen him with any woman but mama. I don't know if we'll like it. If we'll like her."

Trevor nodded. "What made him want to get a new wife so quickly?"

Morgan's mind wandered to the kiss in the bedroom. She closed her eyes for a moment when she was overcome with embarrassment before opening them slowly. "Daddy can't take care of us by his self I guess. Before mama died, she did everything. So I guess Lisa gonna help him out." She sighed. "I told him I can do it but he brushed me off. It ain't like we not getting older." She paused again. "I don't know."

When they reached Morgan's porch, she slipped the key out of her pocket and opened the door. "I think Shaye made some sandwiches. Ya'll go eat and then do your homework. I'll be inside in a minute," she told them.

When they disappeared inside, Morgan closed the door and sat on the porch. The rain hadn't come after all and the sun was peaking through the clouds again.

Trevor sat next to her and wrapped his arm around her shoulder. "I love you, Morgan," he said looking into her eyes. "You the strongest chick I know."

She frowned. "How you figure?"

"I'm serious," he said as he leaned in for a kiss. He nailed it and his lips pressed against hers. "I don't know what it's like to be in your shoes right now," he paused, "you know, with your mother being gone and all. But it's like you stepped up to the plate and did what you had to do. Which is why I want you to know that I'm here for you."

She smiled, looking down and then into his eyes. "Thank you for the compliment but I'm just doing what I gotta." The last thing she wanted was to talk about her mother. "But look, how the college search going?"

"I got a few recruiters checking me out for scholarships." He dropped is hand behind her back and slipped it under her shirt so that he could ease his fingers into the crack of her butt cheeks. College was the last thing on his mind. "But I'd sure hate to go without getting some of that pussy first."

She pushed away from him and stood up. "Stop playing, Trevor." She frowned before looking at the closed door to see if her sisters were watching. "I'm tired of telling you the same thing. I'm not ready to go there with you. When I am, you'll know."

He stood up, brushed the back of his jeans off and bit down on his bottom lip. "Well, when are we gonna go to the next level, Morgan? Huh?" He paused. "Every time I turn around, you pushing me back like I'm some sucka ass nigga. You know how many bad bitches would kill to be in your shoes right now? Do you want me to dump you? 'Cause I will."

Morgan's heart twirled in her chest. Losing him would be the worst thing that could happen right now but sex was the last thing on her mind. "Just give me a few more months and I promise I'll do whatever you want." When he still appeared to be irritated, she gripped his hand. "Just two months, Trevor." She grinned up at him flirtatiously. "I promise I will be worth the wait."

He smiled, stepped back and squeezed her cheek. "Well I hope it's sooner than later. 'Cause I'm getting tired of waiting. I can't stand teases."

He stepped off the porch and walked up the block, leaving her alone.

TWO WEEKS LATER

A cool breeze rolled in through Morgan's open bedroom window. The new stepmother had decided that she wanted to save money in the Collins home so the air conditioner remained off. The sisters tried to dispute the sweltering heat with their father but he said it was for the best, and that Lisa was in charge and they needed to respect her. Morgan felt it was easy for him to say because he was always at work, leaving them alone to deal with the uncomfortable conditions.

When sweat rolled down her face, Morgan wiped it off with the back of her hand as she sat on the floor with Shaye to her right and Petra to her left. Both of them were homeschooled by a professional teacher during the day, due to their erratic behavior. They were unable to attend traditional schools. As she helped them with their homework, Morgan turned her focus back and forth between the two of them until their assignments were complete. Although they had a new stepmother, Morgan was responsible for her sisters because Lisa was uninterested and was hardly ever home herself.

When she was done with them, Lexia entered the room with a fake smile on her face. She wanted something. "Morgan, a few friends are going to—"

"Did you finish your homework?" Morgan asked cutting her off.

"No but—"

"But nothing. You're not about to go to no skate park when you got homework to do!" she yelled. "Now get out of my face, Lexia, and stop asking me questions I already said no to. It's too hot for all of this shit."

Lexia angrily brushed past Grace, who had also entered her sister's room. "What's wrong with her?"

"Nothing," she said standing up before wiping more sweat off her face. "What you need?"

"I wanted to talk to you about this shit that happened in school today." She looked down at Petra and Shaye. "I can come back later though."

Morgan caught on that she wanted privacy and said, "Petra and Shaye, go to your room and finish your homework. I'll be up later to check on you." When they were gone she said, "So what's up?"

"You think I look like a dyke?"

Morgan was stunned at first and stood in front of her sister with her jaw hung and her eyes wide as she waited for her to finish her statement. "Wait…you serious?"

"Yeah," she huffed. "I'm not playing."

"Grace, no you don't look like a dyke. Why you say that?"

"Some girls at school said it and I was five seconds from fighting them but I thought about daddy. With mama gone I don't want him having to worry about me in school, you know?" She paused. "But I did say something out the way and now the teachers want to talk to him."

Although the girls at school didn't know, Morgan was quite aware that her sister could snap so she decided to help her since she obviously showed restraint. That type of behavior needed to be rewarded. "Want me to talk to the teachers? I can fake like I'm your parent. Or better yet, your aunt since I know the school is aware that Mama died. They probably wouldn't even trip with me talking to them. Especially if I say daddy's grieving. "

"That will help me out a lot," Grace grinned and then bopped out of the room.

With her sisters out of the way, she was about to prepare dinner when suddenly she smelled roast and onions. She didn't know anyone was cooking.

"Girls, come downstairs," Hollis yelled. "Dinner's done."

Hollis sat proudly at the head of the table but Morgan couldn't help but notice something fake in his eyes. It was as if he was trying to pretend everything was well and Morgan didn't know how to take it. Was he still mad at her about the night in his room? Was he worried about his new wife and if she would fit in?

When the sisters assembled around the dining room table, Morgan was shocked. Since Lisa had been there, she hadn't said two words to them outside of keep the air conditioner off and use your same cup to drink water.

But now Lisa busied herself with the pots and pans like she was used to this shit. Her auburn hair sat in a tight bun on top of her head and she scratched it every so often as she continued about her work. Morgan couldn't see her face but her body language screamed *this is my job and I will do it to the best of my abilities.* Maybe Lisa wasn't as bad as she let on.

One of the reasons she didn't have a bond with the new stepmother was because the moment

Lisa Collins was introduced to the family, Hollis yanked her out of the house and whisked her off to a small island for a few days. When she came back she was never home and was always detached. But now, since she was cooking, Morgan started to think that maybe things would change for the better.

When the stepmother turned around, placed a royal blue pot of mashed potatoes on the table and smiled brightly at Morgan, suddenly she liked her. There was kindness in her eyes.

Lisa wiped her hands on the towel that hung over her shoulder and tossed it in the corner on a chair, which also held her purse. Morgan did notice that she didn't go anywhere without that bag. "Hello, girls," Lisa said with a wave of her hand. She walked over behind Hollis and placed her palm on his shoulder. "I hope you enjoy the meal. It's been a long time since I cooked roast but I wanted this to be nice. Especially since I've been gone so much lately that we haven't had a chance to get to know one another."

"I'm sure it will be delicious, sweetheart," Hollis said looking up at her. When he looked at his girls, he couldn't gauge their expressions. Did they like her or not? They all seemed stiff at the display.

"I hope so, Hollis," she said before looking at the Collins sisters again. "I'm so happy to be a part of this family and I just want you all to know that I'm going to do whatever I can to make my stay here comfortable." She paused. "For you girls, that is." She smiled. "I know what it is to lose a mother. I lost mine at ten years old. I just wanted you to know that I'm here to be Lisa, not your mother or your boss." Her eyes settled on Morgan's and she smiled brighter.

Morgan was skeptical at first about having a new stepmother but after hearing her statement, she was relieved.

Lisa served everyone and was just about to pray over the meal when Petra pushed back in her seat, stood up and said, "I don't trust this fake bitch!"

The smile on Lisa's face melted away like ice cubes sitting in the sun. "Excuse me?" Lisa said fluttering her eyes.

"I said you're a fake bitch and I don't like you," Petra repeated.

Hollis wiped the corners of his mouth with a napkin and lowered his brow. "Petra Collins, you mind your tongue!" he yelled.

"I'm not listening to you, daddy," Petra said before grabbing her plate. "I hate that bitch and I hate you for bringing her here." She stomped up-stairs and dropped a piece of meat on the way, but picked it up and slapped it back on her plate before continuing the trek to her room.

Hollis hopped up from the table. "Petra Collins, you come back here this instant," he demanded. "Petra!" It soon became obvious that he could yell all he wanted. Petra was already in her room, sitting Indian style on the floor as she ate her dinner. It was best she stayed gone anyway because he knew that if he forced her to come back she would do nothing but give Lisa more of her mind and he didn't want that.

"I'm sorry, honey," Hollis said touching his new wife's hand. "Petra didn't mean to be so cross."

"I understand," she said under her breath. "I just wanted so much…"

Lisa was still talking but Morgan couldn't hear her words anymore. While Hollis consoled her, suddenly Morgan's opinion of the doting wife changed. Petra was a fire starter but she was also a truth talker and if she saw something in Lisa, they all should be afraid.

So Morgan examined Lisa closer. Her eyes rolled over her fingers that clutched Hollis's shoulder hard, as if she were in charge. She observed her jittery stance. And then she looked at her eyes. Something about her was off...way off.

Morgan was still in the examining mood when Lisa's eyes met hers. And that's when Morgan noticed what Petra saw all along. Just beneath the surface of her fake smile was a hint of deceit. Lisa did a good job of concealing it behind the light makeup that brushed her face but it was still there. She had ulterior motives, but what were they?

When Lisa grinned at her as if to say, "Yes, bitch, you need to be worried about me," Morgan's heart rate increased. She was certainly the devil.

Despite the mood change after Petra's exit, the Collins family was able to enjoy the meal. Evil stepmother or not, the food was delicious and Morgan and her sisters devoured it all, especially since it was the first real meal they had since Annie died.

When dinner was done Hollis stood up, wiped his mouth and said, "Well, girls, I have to get to work."

Everyone begged him to stay but he smiled and told them he couldn't.

"Aw, honey. You sure you can't have a slice of apple pie?" Lisa asked holding the entire pie in her hand.

He rubbed his growing belly. "I wish I could." He kissed her cheek. "Just save me a piece. I'm sure I'll get into it when I get home." He hugged his girls, kissed his loving new wife and left.

The moment his double-breasted black jacket walked out of the door, the girls situated themselves in their chairs so that they could bombard Lisa with a thousand questions over pie. Besides, this was the first chance they had to really talk to her since she was never home in the past.

Lexia, always the adventurer, slapped her hands together as if she were trying to keep them warm and said, "So, Lisa, tell me something about yourself." She grinned. "I mean something we don't know already."

Lisa smiled as she continued to cut the pie into eighths. When she was done, she sat the knife down and said, "Why, bitch?" The Collins sisters all gasped. "I'm fucking your father, not you." She wiped her hands on the hand towel that once again hung so effortlessly over her shoulder and tossed it in Lexia's face. "Stay in a child's place and not in my love life."

"I know you didn't just disrespect my sister, bitch," Grace said jumping up. She was fully prepared to crack her jaw but Morgan pulled her back and pushed her into her seat.

"Lisa, what's wrong with you?" Morgan asked, totally stunned by her attitude.

"You mean starting with the fact that my husband got more pussy in this house than a brothel?" she said slyly. "Do me a favor, stay the fuck out of my way and I'll stay out of yours." She released the Bobbi Pins that held her bun in place and allowed her auburn hair to drop down on her shoulders. When Lisa disappeared upstairs in her innocent baby blue dress and came back down in tight jeans and a low cut black top with her titties hung out, they knew being married was the last thing on her mind. She turned the doorknob and said, "Bye, bitches. Don't wait up." She twisted her hips outside and slammed the door behind her.

"I guess Petra was right," Morgan said under her breath.

"You should've let me bust that bitch in the face," Grace said as she stood up and paced next to the table, cracking knuckle after knuckle.

"Grace is right, Morgan. I'm scared now," Lexia said as she looked up at her with tears welling up in her eyes.

"I want daddy," Shaye sobbed as her body trembled. "I want daddy."

Morgan rushed over to Shaye and hugged her. "Everything gonna be alright."

"Why you lying to her?" Grace asked. "Daddy married a monster and she need to know the truth."

"Everybody stop it," Morgan yelled. "Now ya'll got Shaye upset."

"We not the ones who got Shaye upset," Grace corrected her. "Daddy's evil wife did." Grace paused. "Now we need to get Petra down here and find out how she knew something was wrong when we didn't."

Morgan shook her head. "You right." She looked at the stairs and yelled, "Petra, come down here right quick!"

She opened her door and said, "I'm not coming down there unless that bitch is gone!"

"She is!" Morgan responded. "Now come down. We gotta ask you something."

Petra came down the stairs, flicking a white lighter in her hand. She stopped at the foot of the steps, hair as wild and curly as ever. "What up?"

"How you know?" Morgan questioned.

"Know what?"

"That Lisa wasn't a good person."

Petra shook her head in irritation. "Simple. She claimed to be a stepmother but she wore a red bra under her baby blue dress. I also saw a pack of condoms in her purse on the chair."

"And?" Grace said.

"Well if she fucking daddy why she need condoms?"

Morgan was frozen stiff. Mainly because she was surprised that Petra knew so much about sex.

"So what do we do now?" Grace asked Morgan, cracking her knuckles again. "Petra put it down and now we gotta get her up out the house."

Morgan exhaled. "Mama always said a rat will show itself at some point if you patient enough." She paused. "All we gotta do is put some cheese out and watch her come to us. Like mama said, soon all will be revealed."

The next morning, Morgan woke up to a heat so sweltering that everything she wore was soaking wet with sweat. She rolled out of the bed to go to the shower but Lexia was already inside it singing. They took many showers since the air was only on when Lisa wanted it. She was just about to use the bathroom on her father's level when she saw Grace in the doorway talking to Lisa.

Grace understood what her sister meant yesterday about waiting but she had other plans. So while Lisa slid on her makeup in the bathroom mirror, Grace decided to antagonize her.

"I don't like how you talked to my sister yesterday." She cracked her knuckles. "And if you want to keep your health in check, you better be careful what you say to us in the future."

Lisa tossed her brush down and turned around to face Grace. "What you gonna do? Hit me?" She tilted her head. "If you did, what do you think your father would say?" She leaned up against the doorframe and grinned at her. "He would probably put your young ass out on the street. So if you gonna hit me, do it or get the fuck out of my face."

When Morgan saw Grace balling up her fist, she rushed over to her just before she connected with Lisa's nose. "Don't do it, Grace."

Lisa looked at Grace and Morgan, giggled in their faces and proceeded down the steps as her hips switched from left to right in her tight jeans.

"She really don't give a fuck," Grace said as she disappeared. "She's gonna be the death of us. We gotta get her out of here."

The next afternoon, Morgan was walking down the street after meeting Trevor in the park for a kiss session. Her lips throbbed because he sucked on them so hard as he jerked off and they were swollen. Although she was with him for most of the day, her mind was on Lisa. She was trying to figure out, outside of dressing like a whore, what else she had going on. If Morgan didn't come up with a plan she knew Grace and Lisa could come to blows one day.

She was three blocks from her house when she saw long flowing auburn hair hanging out of the back window of a car that looked strikingly like her stepmother Lisa's.

Morgan approached the car and when she was upon it, she saw her stepmother, naked from the waist down. She was on her knees in the backseat while Casual Chris fucked her from behind. He earned the nickname because he always dressed in slacks and a Polo shirt, even when he played basketball at the public court.

Horrified by the sight, Morgan stepped up to the car and knocked hard on the window. When Lisa looked and saw her, she pushed Casual Chris back and tried to hide her ass with his slacks.

"I'm telling daddy!" Morgan promised as she pointed at her. "You ain't nothing but a freak!"

Lisa looked as if she saw a ghost. She got dressed and rushed to catch Morgan before she went into the house. She snatched her forearm. "I'm begging you not to do this."

Morgan could still smell the stench of sex on her. "Get off of me." She yanked her arm away from her. "You don't love my daddy!"

"I do and this would kill him. I'm begging you, Morgan." She paused. "Please let's keep this between us." When Lisa saw that Morgan had no intentions of keeping the indiscretion private, she exhaled. "I know why you're mad."

"What you talking about?"

"You mad because he fucking me and not you."

Morgan felt like she was gut punched. Her stomach tightened and her brow lowered.

"What?"

"He told me you tried to kiss him," she said slyly. "But you will never be enough for him. You will never be what he needs. Keep that in your tiny mind while you think of my pretty face over and over again."

Morgan felt betrayed. Why would Hollis tell a stranger something so private? She wondered who else knew.

Stunned, Morgan stood in place as she watched Lisa switch up the street.

But three days later, she was gone.

CHAPTER FOUR
APRIL 20TH

Dear Diary,

Daddy was sad for two seconds when Lisa left. It made me feel better that she was gone so I never mentioned what I saw her do with Casual Chris. After Lisa, I didn't want another stepmother so I worked harder. I made sure all of my sisters were up bright and early every morning for school and I helped Shaye cook breakfast, lunch and dinner.

But I guess Lisa was right. No matter how hard I worked, I would never be enough.

So he brought in the new stepmother called Joanne.

April 13th

The rain crashed against the window as Grace hustled around her room opening and slamming dresser drawers. "Which one of ya'll took my money?" she yelled. She dropped to her knees and looked under her bed. "I know one of ya'll took it." She rushed out of her room and hit it toward Morgan's room with her fists clenched and arms swinging.

Morgan was shaping up the edge of Shaye's hair so that her cut could remain as low as a teenage boy's when she heard Grace's frantic voice. "What you fussing about now?" She screamed as she sat on the edge of her bed with Shaye sitting on the floor between her legs.

Upon hearing Grace and Morgan, the other Collins sisters stampeded into Morgan's room. They planted themselves in the middle of the room and struck a pose as they waited for the scene to unfold.

Grace rushed into the room seconds later and looked around at her sisters. "One of ya'll stole my money again! This the second time this week! Give it here before I punch everybody in the face."

Lexia was plaiting a braid that unraveled and Petra was scratching her curly fro until they heard Grace accuse them.

Angry at her blaming them for taking her money, Morgan pushed Shaye out of the way and jumped in Grace's face. Grace may have been a threat on the streets but at home there was no one harder than their older sister Morgan. "I know you mad, Grace," she placed both hands on her hips, "but if you accuse your sisters of stealing again I'm gonna snatch your face off."

Grace's arms dropped down by her sides and the scowl wiped away.

"Now tell me what's going on?" Morgan said calmly after regaining control.

Grace exhaled and tried to keep her anger in check. The last thing she needed was to get beat down in front of her sisters. "Before I took a shower today, I hid my money in the back of my bottom drawer. I put it there because last week daddy gave me a fifty dollar bill and it went missing. When I asked everybody but you about it, nobody knew what happened."

"So?" Morgan shrugged. "Maybe you lost your money." She sat back on the bed to finish Shaye's hair. "It's not that big of a deal. Just ask daddy for some more." It wasn't like they didn't have access to paper.

"He out of town at that convention 'til Monday. And I wanted to go to the movies with my friends."

Morgan didn't feel like the madness so she stood up again and stomped toward her drawer. "Damn it, Grace. You can borrow my money. Just give it back when daddy give you yours." Unlike her sisters, Morgan kept her cash in her top drawer, inside of a tiny pink bag, which held her tampons. But when she retrieved the pouch and opened it she saw that her money had also vanished.

Morgan turned around and looked at her sisters.

"Don't look at me," each said shaking their head.

In all of the years Morgan lived with her family, they never had a problem with thievery. She looked at all of them and said, "It's the stepmother. I'm fucking sure of it!"

Grace's face crawled into a frown.

"But why would she do that?" Lexia asked. "Daddy give her money every week like he give us, 'cept she get more."

"I don't know but she gotta go too!" Grace said as she cracked her knuckles.

"Don't nobody do nothing just yet," Morgan said as she paced the room before stopping at the window and looking at the large oak tree in the backyard. "I gotta think of a plan."

For the next few days, the sisters put the stepmother under surveillance. They paid so much attention to Joanne that she was starting to feel a little uncomfortable which was part of Morgan's plan. Joanne was just like Lisa in that she spent most of her time outside the house. Even though she was constantly watched and Morgan instructed her sisters to hide all of their important things, Joanne always managed to get a hold of their money. She was good at it too. She was even able to swipe the fifty-dollar bill that Shaye tucked in her underwear, which she had for years. She cried nonstop for a week until Hollis gave her some more.

When Morgan told Hollis about the missing money, as usual he assumed she was trying to get rid of another stepmother. His exact words were, "Nobody can ever come close to your mother, Morgan. So stop looking for fault and give her a chance."

Morgan realized that if they were going to find out what was up with Joanne, she would have to do it. So while her sisters were out playing, she stayed in the house. While they were busy in their rooms reading or talking on the phone, she kept an eye on Joanne. She still didn't understand where the money was going until one Sunday. She had hung out with Trevor because he hadn't seen her in weeks. But when she stepped into the house, she smelled a sweet funk. Her sisters were at the movies and her father was at work, which meant the stepmother was the cause of the odor.

Morgan walked quietly into the house and into the kitchen. There, sitting on the floor, she saw Joanne. Her back was against the dishwasher and a glass pipe was pressed against her lips. The matted hairstyle Joanne sported that Morgan always thought was a weave lay next to her ashy foot, revealing a tan wig cap underneath.

Joanne Collins, Hollis's third wife, was a crack head.

"Joanne," Morgan whispered. "What are you doing?"

After taking a hard pull, Joanne allowed the pipe to rest at her side. "Please don't tell your father." She was too high to realize the severity of the matter so her words were calm. "This my last time. I promise. Now get over here and hug your mother."

Morgan stepped out of the kitchen backwards and dipped upstairs. She ran into the closet, entered the code to her father's secret safe and removed a gold Rolex watch. Once it was in her hand, she rushed back down the steps and handed it to Joanne whose eyes grew as large as two frying pans when she saw the expensive jewelry. She was a crack head but she was smart enough to know luxury when she saw it.

Holding the watch firmly in her hand, she said, "Take this and never come back. If you stay away I won't bring up the watch 'cause daddy got another one just like it. But if you do come back, I'll tell him that you forced me to give it to you and we'll call the police. I'll cry so good I know the cops will believe me."

A single tear rolled down Joanne's face. She stood up and sat her wig back on her head. "I know this looks bad but I really tried," she said although her eyelids were closing and opening. "I wanted to be a good mother but it's not in me. Maybe that's why all of my children are dead. I lost them when they starved to death, one by one."

Through clenched teeth, Morgan asked, "Where did daddy meet you?"

"An ad on Craigslist," she slurred. "Not sure what's going on with your family but I do know he loves you. And I also know if it's not me, there will be another stepmother." She almost fell over but got herself together. "Consider yourself lucky to have a father who cares about you. If I had a man in my life, I wonder what kind of woman I would be." She paused. "Guess we'll never know." She snatched the watch and walked out of the door.

They never saw her again.

THE MEANEST OF THEM ALL

CHAPTER FIVE
MAY 11TH

Dear Diary

After Joanne left, daddy didn't bring a new stepmother in right away. Instead, he spent more time with us and away from his job.

I liked it!

We got to learn stuff about our father I never knew. Like the fact that he met mama's foster mother before he met her. And that he was in the army for four years. He would sit on the sofa and tell us story after story about his life and I felt like we were getting close all over again.

Until she came.

Dressed up with a pretty face, a big smile and a nice attitude. Everyone thought she was the second coming.

But, unlike when I first met Lisa, I never trusted her.

I could tell by the look in her eyes that she would be the meanest of them all.

🥾 🥾 🥾

May 5th

The television blasted as the Collins sisters sat on the couch and the living room floor watching TV in the afternoon. Whenever they watched *The Real Housewives Of Atlanta,* the sound had to be loud because everyone had an opinion and you couldn't hear what the cast was saying.

Although the sisters were into the show, Morgan was trying to get her thoughts together despite the commotion. She wanted to know where her father was. Earlier, Morgan told the girls she would be ordering pizza but first she had to wait to hear from Hollis. She called him about an hour ago to ask what he wanted on his pie because she knew he didn't like mushrooms or pepperoni but it went straight to voicemail. And he didn't call back. It was so unlike him.

"I'm hungry," Petra said. "When we eating?"

"Like I said, let's give daddy five minutes to call."

"Did you see that?" Grace asked Morgan as she nudged her arm. She was overly excited and normally Morgan would be too but this time was different. "Nene just went off on Kandi. You missed that shit!"

Morgan stood up and walked toward the phone on the wall. Too much time had passed and she decided not to make them wait any longer. "No, I didn't see it. I'll just watch the reunion."

"Well what you thinking about?" Grace asked in a concerned tone.

Morgan was about to place the order for the food. She decided to order a plain cheese pizza for him, knowing that he could never turn that down. But the moment she dialed the number, the front door opened and in walked Hollis.

The sisters, with the exception of Morgan, hopped up to greet him even though the best part of the reality show was coming on. Things had been so good in the Collins home that they missed him when he wasn't around. The girls hugged whichever part of his body they could grab and Petra hung in the background with Morgan until the others got their attention.

When all of the sisters received affection from their father, he looked into each of their eyes. "Sweethearts, I have someone I want you to meet.

Now, I know we've had some problems in the past but it was only because I didn't marry for love. This time I did."

Morgan's heart rate kicked up as if someone was playing drums in her chest. How could he love another outside of their mother?

"So, girls, here she is," he pushed the door open more and the sun was so bright that the only thing Morgan could see was her silhouette in the doorway.

Raising their hands for shade, they squinted and tried to get a better view. The woman stepped further into the house, holding ten bags from different department stores. Her long, light brown hair cascaded down her shoulders and she smiled so brightly Grace, Lexia and even Shaye immediately liked her. They didn't know if she would be a mean stepmother but she certainly was the most beautiful of them all.

However, not all of the Collins sisters were sold so easily. Morgan and Petra elected to save their verdicts for later. Time had proven that Hollis was a bad judge of wives.

"Hello, girls," she said as she smiled brighter. "My name is Roxanne and I'm your new stepmother."

When Petra got a good view of her, she looked her up and down and said, "This bitch is the worst of them all." She ran up the stairs without giving the woman a second thought.

Morgan, who was now hip that Petra, although blunt, knew what she was talking about, decided that she didn't like her either. With a frown on her face, Morgan observed Roxanne closer. And there, right behind the smile, was a ball of hate and deceit. Except unlike when she first pulled Lisa's card, Roxanne remained in character. Her hand was over her heart and her mouth hung open as if her feelings were hurt.

While Morgan was busy checking Roxanne out, Roxanne also noticed something special about Morgan. It was as if they were quietly evaluating the other's mental stamina to see who would rule.

"I'm sorry, sweetheart," Hollis said kissing Roxanne on the cheek. "Petra can be a little hard at times. But I predict that she'll be in love with you before the month's end."

Morgan giggled, knowing that was bullshit. When her father looked at her, she cleared her throat and said, "I'm sorry. I didn't mean to laugh."

"It's no problem, Hollis," Roxanne said. "I expect her to be leery. She doesn't know anything about me. I'll go up there and talk to her later."

Roxanne kissed his cheek and Morgan had one question. Why was her father picking women off the street as if he was plucking apples from a tree? She had no idea that he did the same thing with her mother Annie.

Unlike her family, who lived in a large home, courtesy of their hardworking father and his career in the candy industry, Annie had a rough life. At fifteen years old, she was adopted without ever knowing her mother and father.

When Annie Townsend first moved in with the Martins, a black middle class family from suburbia, she was hopeful that she would have a wonderful life. At the foster home she lived in prior to meeting the Martins, she was physically abused and made to be a servant and when the Martins looked into her eyes, they promised to never treat her so foul.

To build a solid bond with Annie, Karen pulled her to the side to talk to her in private before taking her into their home. She could sense Annie's reluctance about moving with them and she wanted to put her at ease. She had no intentions on hurting her and it was important that she made that clear.

"Annie, you can trust me and my husband," Karen said. "I will always watch over and protect you."

For some reason Annie believed her. It was probably the love she saw when she looked into her eyes and the next week Peter and Karen Martin accepted Annie into their five thousand square foot home and gave her the life of a princess. Each window looked out onto beautiful pea green trees and acres of land. Life radiated from the home and Annie's cozy bedroom offered her a place of security and solitude, which she never had. The Martins and their three sons didn't treat Annie like an outsider, they treated her like family.

Although Annie loved Peter, she was drawn more to Karen. She reminded her of the mother she never had. Annie wasn't the only one who loved Karen. Everyone gravitated toward her because she wore her heart on her sleeve. She helped out a lot of people in the community and even gave money to troubled teens when she saw them in need. Thugs and saints loved her alike and would protect her at all costs.

Life was appreciable for Annie until Karen died of cancer. For a month after Karen's death, Annie and the Martin men were beside themselves with grief. Annie, fearing she might be asked to leave with Karen no longer around, she did all she could to make the men happy. She cleaned after them, cooked their meals and pleaded with them to keep her around. Before long, Peter grew aroused by her begging and he became sexually attracted to her. She was no longer his daughter. She was now a bitch in his house with a wet pussy and he wanted some. Six months later, Peter and his sons told Annie she could stay, if she would agree to be their sex slave.

Fearing homelessness, twenty-year-old Annie agreed. For months she was used sexually and after awhile Peter and his sons couldn't get off on simple intercourse. They needed more so they began physically abusing her too. Annie's glorious lifestyle turned brutal in less than a year and she didn't see happiness in her life anymore. They even took her large room and threw her in the basement.

Annie's once healthy body grew frail and her disposition was flat. She was a walking zombie and before long, she grew numb. As long as she kept her vagina clean, the Martin men didn't care how she felt. It was all about what they wanted. Soon, Annie resigned herself to the fact that her life would forever be bleak.

So there was no way she could see her life being anything but gruesome on the day she met Hollis Collins while on a food run for the Martins. Hollis, a mid-level candy distributor, was at a Chinese carryout restaurant after working forty hours straight. The red haired man with the light skin was at the counter preparing to pay for his beef and broccoli order when he saw Annie. A man of vision, he was able to see her beauty despite her sickly body and face that was covered with hopelessness.

"How much for my food?" Hollis asked the cashier.

"$9.99," she responded.

"Add her meal with mine," Hollis told the cashier.

Annie didn't know what was going on at first because as always, she was looking at the floor.

"Is that okay with you?" the cashier asked. "That he pay for your meal?"

When Annie raised her head and saw Hollis she was as captivated by him as he was by her. He had a freckled face but it worked for him and a smile unrolled on her face but quickly evaporated as if she remembered that she didn't have the right to feel pleasure. She was a lackey and would always be. What was the use in smiling?

"I guess so," she responded returning her eyes to the floor.

Hollis paid for the meal and shook off the fact that she didn't say thank you. He was about to walk out until he leaned in and noticed the flood of bruises on her dark chocolate face. But there was also something about her that was vaguely familiar. Although he couldn't remember it at the moment.

"What happened to you?" he asked as if he had the right to question her about her life. "Is someone beating you?"

Annie took one look at him, grabbed her food and rushed out of the carryout without an answer.

Now Hollis was intrigued. Instead of going to Johnny's house and playing cards like he had been earlier, he decided to follow her home. Something about Annie pulled him to her and he could not walk away. At least not without speaking to her a bit more.

When Annie parked in front of her house Hollis pulled behind her and parked also. He waited patiently for her to get out and when she did he rolled his window down. "Can I have a second of your time?"

Annie was overcome with panic because he was in front of her home. If the Martins saw her keeping time with a man, she couldn't be sure how they would react. The last time she smiled at a mailman, they were so angry they beat her worse than they ever had and locked her in the basement for a week. No food. No water. No light.

"Please leave," she pleaded while clutching the bag that held their food in her hands. "You'll get me in trouble. You don't know how my family can be. I'm begging you."

Hollis lowered his brows. "Who got you this scared?" He paused. "Huh?"

"It's not your place. Now please leave."

"The least you could do is tell me your name."

"Annie," she said hurriedly, hoping he'd leave. "You don't know my family though so you have to get out of here."

"Annie, I don't know if you're married. And if you are I don't know if the man you're with is abusing you. But I do know I can help you if you want. But if you do, you gotta come with me now. I won't be back."

"Why you wanna help me so bad?" She just knew he wanted what the Martin men wanted...sex.

He shrugged. "Because I knew Karen Martin, and if I'm not mistaken, I saw you with her before. I couldn't remember when I first saw you in the restaurant, but I know now." He paused. "She helped me out when I didn't have nobody to look out for me. And I guess I want to return the favor."

Annie cried her eyes out because even though Karen was dead, she kept her promise. She sent someone to protect her. It was as if she had a guardian angel. For the first time in a long time somebody cared to see beyond her scars. Annie knew this was her one moment to escape. So she looked at the big beautiful house that stood behind her and then back at Hollis's large dark brown eyes. Her mind was made up. She dropped the food to the ground, slipped into Hollis's ride and made up her mind to start a new life.

Although he was saving Annie's life, he would also be saving himself too. After all, Hollis, a newly single man, was lonely and couldn't properly take care of himself no matter how hard he tried. His ex-girlfriend, Mandy, decided that she didn't like the late hours he worked and left him for her ex-boyfriend on the day he was celebrating his 22nd birthday. Prior to her leaving, she did everything for him. Made his meals. Cleaned his house and paid the bills with the money he provided. And in her absence the piles of dishes filled the sink and colonies of decaying food sitting on plates in the corners produced a smell that overwhelmed his home. He needed help. He needed a woman's care and love and that's where Annie came in.

Within a month's time, she had his home and his life back on track. Not a morning passed where he didn't smell bacon frying on the stove and fresh biscuits rising in the oven. And when the moonlight shined against his home at night, Hollis was always greeted with a hot meal and fresh baked dessert steaming from the oven. Annie was not lazy and she loved caring for him. She didn't have a job or trade so what else could she do?

After awhile everything was in order except his love life. Being sexually abused for so long, it took her a moment to open her legs for him. But when she did, he took care of her body and she rewarded him with five beautiful daughters who he could call his own. Daughters who were now staring down their mother's replacement.

Instead of worrying about Petra, Roxanne focused on the other sisters who embraced her. "You must be Grace," she said looking over at her.

"How you know my name?" Grace asked seriously.

"Your father told me about your cute bob haircut. Although I must say you are even prettier than he said you were."

Grace blushed.

Roxanne dipped into one of the bags and pulled out a pair of red Beats by Dre wireless headphones. "These are for you. He told me that you like to shut out the sounds around you. So I figured you'd love these."

Grace's eyes widened. She asked her father for a pair two months ago but he said they would ruin her hearing and he refused to buy them. She figured that if Roxanne could get him to change his mind, she was already cool in her book. "Thank you so much," she said taking the gift. "I've been wanting these for so long!"

"You're so welcome, honey."

"I really do appreciate it! I'm about to set these up now!" She dipped up the stairs with the large box in tow.

With Grace taken care of, Roxanne's eyes rolled on to Lexia and she smiled brighter. "You must be the adventurer!" she said excitedly.

Lexia shook her head up and down rapidly as she anticipated her gift. "Yep, that's me!" she yelled proudly.

Roxanne giggled. "Well I hear you love to braid your hair. So I bought you this book on cool natural braiding hairstyles. That way you can be one step ahead of them chicks at your school." She pulled out a beautiful, big hardback book on braiding. To some, the gift may have seemed weak but Lexia was not only an adventurer but she also loved reading and exploring worlds outside of her own.

Lexia grabbed the book, pressed it against her chest and said, "Oh my goodness! Thank you so much! I love it!"

One by one, Roxanne was dismantling her sisters' snake sensors and Morgan feared she and Petra would be the only sensible ones left. It was obvious that she already had Hollis, which was the main reason she was still there.

"Now you must be Shaye," Roxanne said looking at the shy child.

Shaye nodded and hid behind Morgan's back.

That's right, be careful about this bitch, Morgan thought.

"Well your father told me that you love to cook. Is that true?"

Shaye nodded again and stepped from behind her sister. Now she had her too.

"Well, I figured you would love what I have in here." Roxanne dipped into the bag and pulled out one red and one blue cupcake pan. Then she reached back into the bag and pulled out vanilla cake mix with chocolate icing. "Now I figured you and I could bake tonight. That is, if it's okay with you."

Shaye nodded her head up and down and a smile spread so wide on her face her cheeks rose in the air. "Yes," she said in a low voice. Roxanne could barely hear her. "That's okay with me."

With everyone taken care of and Petra upstairs, Roxanne focused on the true matriarch of the family. The one who she was sure pulled the strings around the Collins home. Winning Morgan over would be tough but she felt up for the task. "And you must be Morgan."

Morgan nodded but her expression was bare. She wanted her to know that none of that fancy footwork she pulled on the others would work on her. If she wanted to win her over, she had better come hard. She had better treat her sisters' right and she had better do right by her father.

Roxanne, who loved a challenge, reached into her pocket and Morgan was instantly insulted. Each of her sisters had big gifts, yet her present was tiny enough to fit in her pocket.

Roxanne, unaware of what Morgan was thinking, continued to push into her pocket until she pulled out a set of keys. She reached for Morgan's hand and said, "Come with me. I have something to show you."

Morgan's heart thumped around in her chest. This could not be the day she always dreamed of. It just couldn't. But when she stepped out of the house and saw the brand new black Honda Accord, she knew that it was.

This stepmother was good.

She was really good.

And that scared Morgan even more.

"I told your father that at seventeen years old, you need a new car," Roxanne said softly. "Now he gave me a hard time at first," she said as she looked up at him and winked, "but I told him that you sounded responsible. He told me about how much you do for your sisters and how you walk everywhere you go. I think you are responsible enough to drive. Besides, it's not like he hasn't taught you how to operate a car already." She handed her the keys. "I hope you like it."

Morgan was so excited she was stiff. To an outsider it would look like she was ungrateful but she did appreciate the amazing gesture. All of her young life she wanted a car and yet the new stepmother had done what her own mother couldn't get Hollis to do.

"Do you like it?" Roxanne asked hopefully.

Morgan turned around and observed her pretty face. Instead of being overjoyed, she feared her more than she did all of the wives before her. If this woman could make her father break one of his cardinal rules, what else could she get him to do?

"I love it," she said softly.

"Good, Morgan," Roxanne said excitedly as she clapped her hands together. "Because you and I are going to be the best of friends. I can feel it!"

TWO DAYS LATER

Morgan's room buzzed like Grand Central Station as her sisters ran in and out, each with problems of their own. Although Roxanne was there, you would not have known it because business in the Collins residence went on as usual. It was a school day so one by one the younger sisters filed into Morgan's room with their requests. And although Morgan was on it as usual, she didn't know that this time she had an audience.

Roxanne stood in Morgan's doorway with a fixed smile on her face. She'd been there for fifteen minutes as she contemplated where her place was in the family. Because it was obvious that as of now the real boss was Morgan. All of the gifts, all of the smiles and compliments Roxanne gave them about how pretty they were had expired and now she was looking for another way in.

"Can you braid the front tighter?" Lexia asked as she ran her fingers over the front of her hair. "They keep falling out."

"That's because you want them big," Morgan said. "The smaller ones might not look right but they'll stay."

"I think the big ones look nice too," Roxanne said to Morgan. "I can show you a trick to make them stay longer, Morgan, if you want to learn. I don't mind teaching you."

Morgan looked up from Lexia's head and said, "I got it, Roxanne. Thanks though."

Although Morgan didn't know she was present before, she was aware now and she was uncomfortable with her stares. It wasn't like Hollis wasn't home. So why was she in her room?

When she finished Lexia's hair she said, "Don't go outside and get hurt again."

"That was last week," Lexia said standing up to walk to the mirror and check her braids. "I'm fine now."

"I'm serious, Lexia. One of these days you're going to break more of your bones and daddy's heart in the process. This family can't take another tragedy."

"Okay, Morgan, damn," Lexia responded, eager to go outside to catch up with her friends. "I won't be out long and I won't get hurt either."

When Lexia approached the door Roxanne said, "Your hair is really pretty. I love it."

"Thank you," she responded as she bolted out of Morgan's room.

Morgan didn't get a second's rest before Grace entered with her dilemma. "Can I talk to you?"

"Please don't tell me you got in trouble at school again," Morgan said placing her hands on her hips.

"Then I guess I won't say nothing then," she replied looking at the ground.

"What happened, Grace?"

Grace looked back at Roxanne. "Don't worry," Roxanne responded. "I'm one of the cool kids. I won't say a word to your father." She came further into the room and sat on the floor. Then she pulled her knees against her breasts as if she were a teenager about to hear some juicy gossip. Morgan wanted to throw up.

Damn I wish this bitch just beat it, Morgan thought.

Grace exhaled, looked down at Roxanne and shrugged. "Remember I was telling you about them chicks who tried to jump Nikki at school?" Morgan nodded, knowing her best friend. "Well they called their big sisters up to the school to jump her today and I got involved."

Morgan shook her head. "By get involved you mean you fought them?"

"Yeah, and I'm suspended from school."

Morgan looked down at Roxanne, still unsure if she could trust her. "I already said I'm not going to say a word," Roxanne assured both of them. She crossed her heart. "Scout's honor."

Since she already heard enough anyway, Morgan said, "I'll call your school again. When you home during suspension, just stay out of daddy's way. The last thing we need is him seeing you here when you should be at school"

"Thank you," Grace said.

"Thank nothing. You got kitchen duty for two weeks, Grace. And bathroom duty too. Now get out."

The moment Grace left, Shaye scampered into the room. She scratched her head and whispered, "Somebody drank the milk I was going to use to bake a cake."

Morgan was thoroughly annoyed now. She told the girls repeatedly to leave everything on the right side of the refrigerator alone because those things belonged to Shaye. Shaye didn't ask for much but supplies to bake with and they couldn't even give her that. "Don't worry about it," Morgan sighed. "I'll run to 7-Eleven in a minute and pick you up a half pint."

"Thank you," she whispered before walking out.

No sooner than Morgan thought she would get a moment's rest did Petra tramp into the room in her usual grumpy mood. "I'm hungry," she pouted. She stood in the middle of the floor with her arms folded over her chest. When she saw Roxanne on the floor she rolled her eyes. "What we eating?" She scratched her wild curly hair.

"I'll help Shaye start dinner in an hour." She plopped on the bed. "I just need an hour."

"Come on, Morgan! I might not be alive in an hour."

"You'll live, Petra! Damn. Now get out of my room."

"Stupid bitch," Petra yelled before stomping out of the room, stepping on Roxanne's pinky finger in the process. She continued about her way without even apologizing.

"Ouch," Roxanne yelled.

"Sorry about that," Morgan said although she was happy Petra did it. "I don't think she saw you," she lied.

She stood up and brushed the back of her long skirt off. "Don't worry about it. She'll warm up to me later." Roxanne leaned against the wall. "But I want to talk about you. You seem to have your hands full around here."

Morgan sighed because she was exhausted. In her mind, she didn't have a choice. If she didn't step up she worried that no one would. It was her responsibility to take care of the sisters. "I'm used to it now but sometimes I wish I could have a break."

Roxanne's eyes widened. "I was going to suggest the same thing. I'm here for a reason, Morgan. I didn't just marry your father. I married you girls and I don't want you to be afraid to use me."

Morgan was whipped but she wasn't prepared to relinquish her power. She enjoyed helping her sisters and outside of hanging with Trevor, she wasn't sure what she would do without the responsibility. "Don't worry," she responded as she took a deep breath. "I have things under control with my sisters. You just take care of daddy. And make sure he's happy."

Her comment was off-putting seeing as though she was a child but Roxanne let it ride. "How do you like your new car?" Roxanne asked as she picked up a bottle of peach body spray that sat on Morgan's dresser. "I hardly ever see you drive it. And considering how much your father said you begged him for it, I would think you'd be in it a bit more."

Morgan felt she was trying to throw what she did for her in her face, which was one of the reasons she thought about refusing the gift. But the desire to be a teenager with access to a car trumped her pride so she kept it. However, to make Roxanne think she wasn't interested, she never drove the car when she was home. "Not sure why I don't ride it much but I do like it. Thank you again for buying it for me."

Roxanne sat the perfume down and looked at her slyly. "Morgan, if we are going to be good friends you should start by not lying to me."

"I'm not lying."

"Then it must be a mistake. Because you and I both know that every time you leave the house, your car goes with you. "

Morgan was about to respond when she saw Lexia climbing the oak tree in the backyard. She rushed toward the window, pulled the blinds back and pushed open the window. Lexia was on the highest branch when Morgan yelled, "Lexia, get down from there now and come here!"

Lexia looked toward her sister. "I was just trying to—"

"Get in here now!"

Five minutes later Lexia was in Morgan's room. Morgan stopped pacing and addressed her roughly. "I told you not to climb that tree and you don't listen. So from here on out you'll be on punishment until I tell you otherwise."

"But I was supposed to go to the roller derby—"

"I don't care, Lexia," Morgan said cutting her off. "You should've thought about that before you did what I asked you not to do. Now go to your room!"

Lexia stomped out crying. Roxanne looked out the door behind her and then focused back on Morgan. "Wow, that went very well."

Irritated, Morgan placed her hands on her hips and said, "Roxanne, let me handle my sisters. Besides, they don't do well with new stepmothers. Trust me, we've had our share around here and so far I haven't seen anything impressive." She grabbed her science book and plopped on the bed.

"Now if you'll excuse me I have homework to do before I go to the store and get milk for Shaye."

Roxanne didn't leave right away. Instead, she took a few moments to consider Morgan's attitude. When she finally left she had one mission in mind and it was to bring the self-righteous bitch to her knees.

↳ ↳ ↳

"I hate that black bitch. She not even my mother," Lexia screamed as she wept into her pillow. She planned to go to the roller derby all week and she hated Morgan for ruining the Saturday for her. What was she going to tell her friends? "I hope she get run over by a car and dies!"

When there was a soft knock at her door, she ignored it but it grew louder. If it was Morgan she wanted nothing else to do with her for the rest of her life.

"It's me," she whispered. "Roxanne. May I come in?"

Confused about what she wanted, Lexia sat up straight in bed, wiped her eyes and said, "Come in."

Roxanne stepped into the room and sat on the edge of her bed. She placed a hand on her leg and said, "How do you feel, sweetheart?"

She wiped her nose with the back of her hand and said, "I'm fine." She smiled lightly. "Thanks for asking."

"Your sister hurt your feelings pretty bad, didn't she?"

She nodded. "Yes."

"I was so surprised to hear her talk to you like that," she instigated. "It shocked me."

"You were there?"

"Yes," she said as she slid a few braids behind Lexia's ear. "I hadn't left her room yet." She paused. "I might be new to the family but I don't like how she spoke to you. And it won't be tolerated as long as I'm in charge. You are a human being with feelings and Morgan should take care to understand that."

Lexia sniffled. "I know. And the only thing she does is get on everybody's nerves," Lexia said, pleased someone was seeing things her way. "She thinks just 'cause mama died that she the boss of us. But she not."

Roxanne put her hand over her heart in mock astonishment. "Well she definitely shouldn't think that because she's a child." She leaned in. "Now listen, I don't know what your sister's problem is but I will say this. I'm the stepmother in this family and if you want to climb the tree you can do that. And I'm taking you off punishment too. Okay?"

A smile spread across Lexia's face before vanishing. She realized what Roxanne just said. "No that's okay." She lay back down.

"Don't worry about it, Lexia. You won't get in trouble."

"Ms. Roxanne, I appreciate it but I don't go against my sister," she responded. "I just gotta stay on punishment until she changes her mind. Thank you though."

"I understand, honey." She stood up. "It's good that you girls stick together. Well, I'll let you rest before dinner."

Roxanne moved toward the door. She was smiling on the outside but she was furious on the inside. Morgan held more power over her sisters than she realized. She had to come up with another plan.

The next morning Roxanne woke up early preparing to cook breakfast but to her surprise,

Morgan was in the kitchen already. The sisters were at the dining room table eating bowls of cereal and the scrambled eggs Morgan helped Shaye cook sat in the middle of the table along with strips of bacon.

"Good morning," Lexia said to Roxanne. She looked at her and smiled to let her know that what she said to her in the room would stay between them. "Did you want something to eat? We have more."

"No," she whispered. "I'm…I'm fine. Thanks for asking. You girls just enjoy your meal." Roxanne focused on Morgan who was grinning in her direction.

"Okay, girls," Morgan said standing up from the table. "Hurry up and eat so you can make it to school on time." She looked at Petra and then Shaye. "And you two need to grab your workbooks for Mrs. Hayes. She'll be here in a minute. I hope you did your homework."

A few more days passed and still Roxanne could not find a way to fit into the family. Morgan did a good job of taking care of all of her sisters' needs and protecting them from a stepmother who she felt wouldn't be around much longer anyway.

It was clear that everyone had their own lives in the Collins residence. Hollis was always at work.

Shaye was always baking. Petra spent a lot of time in the backyard digging and playing in the dirt. Lexia spent most of her time with her friends when she got off of punishment early. Grace stayed with her best friend Nikki, who Roxanne assumed she was fucking. And Morgan spent her time guarding them from Roxanne.

Feeling as if there was nothing for her to do, Roxanne decided to take a nap on the recliner in the living room. She was reading one of her favorite books and figured she'd take a quick nap before waking up to finish it. But when she felt tiny bugs crawling all over her body, she abruptly awakened.

Horrified, her eyes popped open and she saw that she was sprinkled with dirt. Roxanne hopped up screaming and ran up the stairs. She slapped and scratched at her face while yelling all the way to the bathroom. When she reached the bathroom mirror she saw red fire ants all over her face and shoulders. Hysterical, she turned the shower on and jumped in with all of her clothes on. She scrubbed her body so hard her skin started bleeding and was raw to the touch.

When she stepped out of the shower, now naked, Petra was standing in the bathroom doorway. "Are you okay?" she asked with a sly smile. "I heard you screaming and stuff."

Roxanne walked up to her with clenched fists but Petra didn't move. "Did you do that to me, you little fucker?" Roxanne yelled stepping toward her. "Huh?"

"I don't like you, stepmother," Petra responded. "I want you to leave before it gets worse." Petra walked out slowly, leaving her in the doorway alone.

Roxanne stared out of the window as she thought about what was happening to her life. The Collins sisters reminded her of her last husband's daughters and she hated them just the same. The Hunter twins did all they could to get her away from their father too.

Roxanne Berry married 40-year-old Donte Hunter when she was twenty-four years old. After suffering five miscarriages in her young age, a doctor finally told her that she could not have kids. Since she was an orphan from birth, having kids was the only way she thought she would have a family of her own. The devastating news had her wanting to take her own life and then she met Donte.

He was newly separated at the time and when his wife died due to a bad drug interaction, he sued the hospital and was awarded two million dollars. But even with all of his money, he was still a man who needed help with his girls.

Immediately Roxanne did all she could to win the fourteen-year-old twins over. From buying them gifts to giving them compliments and attempting to be the cool mom, nothing she ever did seemed to work. Before long, she resented the girls and their father who always brushed off her emotions as if they didn't matter. So she decided to leave. Violently.

For two weeks she instigated a major conflict between Donte and his next-door neighbor Alex. When Donte would come home, she would tell him that Alex complained that the girls were in his yard or playing ball too close to his house. Then she would go to Alex's house and tell him that Donte was complaining that Rex, Donte's friendly neighborhood poodle, was releasing his bladder in the garden and ruining his flowers.

Soon they were engaged in a heated dispute and nobody was calm enough to realize that Roxanne started it all. The dispute took on a life of its own and Roxanne began recording the fights to show the police. She was building her case and was brilliant at it too.

After her work was done and the two hated each other to the point of threatening murder, she got up one night while the Hunters slept, doused the house with gasoline and set it on fire. The entire family died inside.

After a yearlong trial for the Hunter family murders, Alex was finally convicted. The tapes Roxanne presented as evidence ended up being his demise. And Roxanne Hunter walked away a million dollars richer. She was at a bar enjoying her newfound single status when Hollis, with his smooth personality and hefty pockets, approached her. After hanging out with her a few nights, he asked her to be his wife and she said yes. Hollis didn't believe in a long dating game. He wanted what he wanted.

Roxanne rolled on her side and continued to look out into the room. She would not let some irritating little girls push her out of her home. She loved living with Hollis. Money flowed and he took such good care of her that she didn't have to spend her cash. In fact, the biggest item she bought was Morgan's car even though she immediately regretted it.

Roxanne ran her hand over her swollen and bumpy face. Since they wanted to play dirty, she would get dirty too. She was done being Mrs. Nice Mother.

She was considering a plan when Hollis walked into the room. He wasn't aware of what Petra did so he smiled at his wife and headed toward the dresser to remove his watch until he saw her face. "Honey, what happened to you?" He asked as he rushed over toward her. "Look at your face." He touched her cheek with his cool hand. Hollis cared about her even if he didn't love her yet. And Roxanne knew it.

"It's nothing," she sighed. "Just allergies." She continued playing the martyr.

"Sweetheart, are you sure you're okay?" he asked looking into her eyes. "Can I get you anything?"

"I'm positive, Hollis. Please try not to worry. I took a few Benadryl and I should be fine in no time."

He exhaled, leaned over and placed a tiny kiss on her forehead before walking over to the dresser. "So what else is on your mind, honey?" he took his watch off and placed it down. "The girls aren't bothering you, are they?" he joked, although he was half-serious.

THE *MEANEST* OF THEM ALL

Roxanne crawled out of bed. "No, but—" She dropped in the middle of the floor and gripped her forehead. "Oh my God!"

Hollis ran toward her. "What's wrong, Roxanne?"

"My migraines," she cried. "I guess they're back."

"I didn't know you had them."

"I've suffered from them all of my life." He helped her back into bed and placed a few pillows behind her head. "But they only bother me when—"

"You're stressed," he sighed placing the sheet under her chin.

"Yes, sometimes stress does cause them."

"I'm going to have to talk to the girls," he said seriously. He knew his daughters could be a mess and he was pretty sure that they had something to do with the last two stepmothers leaving. He wasn't in love with either of them, though, so it was no real loss. "They can be a harsh if I don't get involved, baby."

"Please don't, Hollis. I really want to do this on my own. And if you get involved they won't trust me. They'll start thinking that I always come to you."

"Okay, but let me give you some information that may help you work things out with my girls. Lexia is a caring person who only wants to see the world and have a good time. Appeal to her sensitive side and you'll win her over easily. Grace is overprotective of her family." He chuckled. "Actually, she's overprotective of everyone. As long as she knows you mean the family well," he paused and touched her face again, "which I know you do, she'll come around. Now, Shaye is easy."

"Yeah, all she wants to do is cook," she giggled. "I have her down pat."

"Exactly." He laughed. "If you spend a little time with her in the kitchen, she'll be your friend for life."

"What about Petra?"

"Petra is a different breed," he sighed. "She won't come around until she's ready so it's best you leave her alone."

Roxanne nodded. "And Morgan?"

"Morgan is a caregiver. When her mother died she took it the hardest. She was in the car when it happened. But Morgan is also smart. Like Petra, with time, she'll grow to love you too. I think with her, it's all about trust."

Hollis had no idea that he just gave Roxanne the key to his family. With the data he'd given her, she was now ready to attack and she would start with Lexia.

The next day, Roxanne moped around the house and left the girls alone. Her red, puffy face along with her somber mood had all of the sisters, except Morgan and Petra, feeling sorry for her. They knew Petra was responsible for the ant attack and since Roxanne was the first stepmother who bought them gifts instead of taking from them, the guilt was overwhelming. And since she didn't tell their father that Petra was responsible, it made them trust her even more. All of these things were part of Roxanne's plan.

Five days later Roxanne was sitting on the recliner with an ice pack resting on her forehead. On the floor, several pill bottles sat at her feet. When the door opened and Morgan and the other Collins sisters came in and saw the condition she was in, their mouths dropped.

Morgan hung in the background and folded her arms over her chest.

"Are you okay, Roxanne?" Lexia asked as she dropped her book bag and ran up to the recliner. She stood on her knees.

"I feel awful," Roxanne whimpered as she touched the top of her hand. "I'll be fine though."

"But what's wrong?" Lexia persisted. "Are you still feeling bad from the allergic reaction you had?" Lexia looked back at Petra, who had just come down the stairs with Shaye, and rolled her eyes. Lexia wasn't with what she did to the step-mother at all.

"Just bad headaches," Roxanne lied. "I'll be fine though." She touched the side of her face.

"We have some stuff in the medicine cabinet upstairs," Grace offered. "Want me to go get it?"

"That's okay," she smiled. "I have plenty medications here. But thanks for being concerned. I really appreciate you girls." She leaned back in the seat and said, "Oh, I almost forgot. I'm ordering pizza tonight." She looked over at Shaye. "That is, if it's okay with you."

"It's fine," Shaye whispered as she played with her fingernails. "I love pizza."

And just like that, Roxanne succeeded in winning over Shaye, Lexia and Grace. When the girls were responding to her, Roxanne winked at Morgan and Petra, out of view of the others.

Days went by and Roxanne was getting closer to the sisters, especially Lexia who even took to calling her ma. Morgan was beyond frustrated. Roxanne wasn't just pushing herself into her sisters' lives, she was tearing them apart. It had gotten to a point where the stepmother was spending more time with them than they were spending with Morgan and Petra.

Roxanne cooked with Shaye every other day. She went on bike rides with Lexia and talked to Grace for hours at a time about her best friend, whom she now knew was her girlfriend, although she didn't tell anyone else. Roxanne was not only a mother; she had become a best friend to each of them.

One day Morgan and Petra were outside in the backyard. They could hear the other sisters and the stepmother inside laughing. "What we gonna do?" Petra asked as she struck matches, blew them out and threw them in the grass.

Morgan looked at the house. "I don't know. But why do you do that shit?"

"Do what?"

"Play with matches?" Morgan nervously stared at the flames as they appear and disappear.

"Because I like them," she shrugged. "Anyway, maybe you should talk to them alone. They always listen to you."

Morgan focused back on her. "I don't know if you been looking but lately nobody listens to me."

"That's 'cause you not playing Roxanne's game." She struck two matches at the same time and blew them out. "You gotta speak from the heart. They'll hear you."

Morgan watched Petra strike a whole box of matches as she considered what she said. Although Petra was weird, she was right. Nobody knew the sisters better than Morgan so if she wanted to get through to them, she had to go deeper. So later on that night when the girls were brushing their teeth and tying their hair scarves, she called a meeting. All of her sisters stood in the middle of her room as she prepared herself to make a speech.

"What do you want?" Grace asked yawning. She rubbed her eyes. "I'm tired. Plus me and Nikki going to the movies tomorrow and I want to get some rest."

"Yeah what's up, Morgan? I'm beat too," Lexia added.

Shaye sat on the floor next to Morgan's feet.

Morgan swallowed and struggled with what to say. It was as if she didn't know her family. She wanted to be honest with her sisters but she also didn't want to appear like Roxanne threatened her. "What do you think mama would say if she saw us not spending time with each other? And not sticking together?"

Grace and Lexia looked at one another. "What are you talking about?" Grace frowned. "We always together."

"No we aren't. Ya'll with each other but you haven't been with me and Petra at all. We sisters and every time we try to kick it with ya'll, you make excuses. I feel like you're letting the stepmother come between us."

"So just because we think the stepmother is nice, we letting someone come between us?" Lexia asked. "That's not fair!"

"Yeah, Morgan," Grace said. "That's not right. She's not like the others. You should give her a chance instead of being so mean and nasty."

Morgan sighed. "Okay, if you feel like you're not doing anything wrong then keep on doing what you're doing. Petra and me won't bother you. As a matter of fact, forget I ever said anything," Morgan slid in bed and pulled the sheets up to her neck. "I bet mama is rolling over in her grave right now. You know how she was about us being together before she died. But ya'll can leave now. I'm sorry I wasted your time." She turned on her side, away from the girls.

The sisters looked at one another and then walked solemnly out of the room. Petra was the only one who stayed behind.

"You think it worked?" Morgan asked, turning back to face her.

Petra grinned mischievously. "I would be really surprised if it didn't."

The next day, Morgan sat on the sofa with Trevor and Petra watching Family Feud. Grace and Lexia sat at the dining room table doing their homework while Shaye made hot chocolate with milk on the stove.

When the front door opened Roxanne was holding two hands full of shopping bags. "Hello, girls," she sang before closing the door. She raised the bags slightly. "I come bearing gifts." She walked over to the dining table with the usual sway in her hips. She smiled at Lexia, Grace and Shaye. She also acknowledged Petra and Morgan but she rolled her eyes at them. No one needed a rocket scientist to know that she didn't have shit in the bag for those two. "So who wants to be first?"

Grace looked at Morgan and Petra before focusing on Roxanne. "Stepmother, I don't want any gifts," Grace said under her breath while looking at her math book. "You've given me enough."

"Yeah, you don't have to give me anything either," Lexia added. "Grace is right. You bought us enough as is." Lexia looked over at Morgan and Roxanne followed her gaze.

The moment Roxanne's eyes rested on Morgan's smirk, she wanted to murder her for turning them against her. Little did the child know, she had just awakened a monster.

🥾 🥾 🥾

Hollis stood in the corner of his room with Roxanne's head between his palms as she gave him a serious blowjob. Her tongue ran up and down the shaft before it wagged back and forth on the tip. Every time she hit the top she stiffened her tongued an eased it into his pee hole. She could taste the saltiness of his pre-cum but she didn't care. She was on a mission.

Hollis was overwhelmed at the skill of his young wife but he tried his best to handle it. Right before he was about to cum, she stopped and looked up at him. "Say you love me."

"I love you," he said once her mouth returned to his stiffness. He hated when women played games with his dick.

"Say you will do anything for me."

"I will do anything for you, baby," he said as he pushed his dick into the warmth of her mouth again.

"Say I'm in control of you."

"What?" he frowned.

"You heard me," she said licking the shaft again. "Tell me I'm in control of you. And say it loudly too."

Hollis wanted to nut so bad that he obeyed her, never knowing that she had ulterior motives. Besides, the moment he came home, she followed him upstairs to seduce him and since the girls were not in the living room he assumed they were asleep. But Roxanne knew the truth and she wanted Morgan to hear who held the real power.

"You're in control of me," Hollis said. "Always."

"That's what I wanted to hear, daddy."

Roxanne continued to suck him hard and Hollis shot his nut down her throat. She swallowed every bit of it. She got exactly what she wanted from him.

Upstairs, standing in the middle of her room holding a framed picture of her mother, Morgan heard it all. She only hoped that her father didn't mean it.

CHAPTER SIX
JUNE 10TH

Dear Diary,
I don't know what happened. One minute things were getting better between me and my sisters and the next they act as if they hate me. Now I'm starting to feel hate for them too.

Maybe it's because nobody talks about mama around here anymore. It hurts too much, I guess.

And the stepmother makes me miss her more. All she wants is to tear us apart.

June 7th

Morgan popped out of bed when she realized she almost overslept. It was the last day of school and she had to get her sisters together or she would be forced to drive them. When her feet touched the floor, she rubbed her throbbing temples. Before getting up, she took a second to recall the events from last night. Once second she was drinking hot tea and the next she was out cold. Why was she so tired? She'd never been that exhausted before.

After resting for a moment, she grabbed her pink robe off the back of the door and walked into the hallway to get everyone up. "Grace!" she yelled rubbing her head again. "Lexia! Are ya'll up? It's time to get ready for school." She would worry about Petra and Shaye later since they were home-schooled.

When no one answered her call, she walked downstairs and was surprised to see Grace and Lexia huddled on the sofa giggling. They were dressed and their hair was in order. Normally Morgan would have to disapprove some of their clothing because what they chose was either dirty or too revealing. But not only were their selections right, they were wearing new gear. "Why didn't ya'll wake me up?" Morgan asked. "I could've helped you get ready for school."

They stopped giggling amongst themselves when they saw how upset she was. "We didn't want to wake you," Lexia said before giggling again. "So we let you sleep."

"Why?"

"Roxanne told us not to bother you," Grace said. "Especially after what you did last night. You were certainly in rare form."

"What happened?" Morgan repeated.

"You were drunk," Lexia whispered. "You got into daddy's scotch. You kept dancing around the house with your t-shirt on asking everybody to look at your stuff. Please don't lie and say you don't remember that shit."

Morgan's face was flushed with embarrassment. "I didn't ask anybody to look at my stuff."

"You did. Roxanne has it on video and everything," Grace continued.

"But all I drank was tea." Lexia and Grace looked at each other in disbelief. Morgan sighed and said, "Where is she?" through clenched teeth. She was sure that the tea Roxanne gave her was filled with liquor.

"Upstairs with Shaye," Grace said. "She hired a new home school teacher who doesn't start until next week. So she's helping her with some other assignments."

"What about Petra?" Morgan continued.

"You know she got mad when she heard about the new teacher. So she in the backyard lighting matches."

"Look, I know you both probably don't believe me but she put some liquor in my shit. I wouldn't mess with daddy's stuff. You know that." Morgan studied their faces to see if they believed her. "I mean, when have you ever seen me act like that?"

Grace and Lexia stood up and grabbed their book bags. "I'll see you later," Grace said under her breath. "Try not to be so hard on Roxanne."

"Yeah, like we said, she's really cool," Lexia added. "She even said she wasn't telling daddy how you were acting or nothing." They both walked out.

Morgan was driving after school with her sisters on her mind. Trevor was in the car and he was tight lipped. Any other day she would ask him was something wrong but she didn't feel like it today. "Have you given any thought to what we talked about?" he asked. "At the movie theater?"

Morgan made a left onto his street. "What did we talk about?"

"Sex."

Morgan was still in her head so she didn't hear what he said. "Morgan," he yelled. "Did you hear me?"

She turned around and saw the anger on his face before focusing back on the road. "I'm sorry, Trevor. My mind is all over the place right now."

"And so is mine. It seems like every time I turn around, you thinking about your sisters. What about us?" He paused. "What about me? You know I got chicks who want to be with me, right?"

She exhaled as she pulled in front of his house. "I know you do because you tell me all the time! Look, if you want to be with them THOTS so bad, then be with 'em and leave me the fuck alone! It's not that big of a deal, Trevor."

Silence.

"Is that what you really want?" he asked.

She exhaled. "No, of course I don't. I just need a little more time, Trevor. And for you not to press me so much. That's all I'm asking. You don't know what it's like having to protect your sisters. "

He pushed the car door open and rushed into his house. She started to follow him but she had to get home to talk to her father before he left for work. When she made it to the house, she was happy when she saw his car out front. So she parked, rushed inside and jogged up the stairs. He was putting his tie on and she was relieved he was still home. One more minute with Trevor and she might have missed him. "Daddy," she said out of breath. "You about to leave?"

He saw his daughter's frightened face and rushed toward her. "What's wrong, honey? You didn't get into an accident, did you? I told you I didn't want you driving that car!"

"No, daddy." He sighed in relief. "It's nothing like that. It's about Roxanne. I think she's trying to turn the sisters against me. I had some tea the other night and she—"

Hollis frowned and walked back over to his dresser. "Morgan, this bickering has to stop. Do you hear what I'm saying? It has to stop and I'm expecting you to be the bigger person." He slid on his watch. "The girls are going to follow your lead. So lead them the right way."

"But she's mean and she doesn't like me."

Hollis sprayed cologne on his wrist and looked at his daughter through the mirror. "Morgan, Roxanne is the head of this family now. And I need you to stand back. I need you to obey her and I need you to stop trying to turn the girls against her." He turned around and looked at Morgan. "Am I clear?"

Later on that day, Morgan was in her bed taking a nap, although it was difficult to fall asleep. The day started out terrible when she confronted Roxanne about getting her drunk and she denied it. Morgan decided to leave it alone because she knew her father wouldn't believe her anyway.

When she rolled over after waking up, Grace was walking into her room. Morgan sat up straight in the bed and said, "What's up?"

"Lexia here yet?" Grace asked stuffing her hands into her pockets.

Morgan rubbed her eyes. "Not that I know of. Why?"

"Because she—"

"Roxanne, help!" Lexia yelled from downstairs. "Help me! Please!"

Morgan and Grace rushed toward the voice and when they made it downstairs they saw Lexia sitting on the floor, holding her ankle.

Roxanne rushed past Morgan and Grace and dropped to the floor with Lexia. "What's wrong, sweetheart?"

"I fell down at the skate park," Lexia cried, holding her leg. "I think it's broke." She was trembling so hard her hair shook.

Morgan stepped up and looked down at her with both hands on her hips. "What were you doing at the skate park, Lexia?" she yelled. "I told you not to go there! Didn't I? Now look!"

"First off, lower your voice," Roxanne responded. "You are not in charge of this family. I am," she said, hoping Morgan would remember how her father yelled out who the boss was during oral sex. "Now, I told her she could go. And accidents happen all the time so relax." Roxanne focused back on Lexia. "Listen, honey, I'm going to raise your ankle, okay? If you're in a lot of pain let me know and I'll put it down and we'll go to the hospital."

"Please don't hurt me," Lexia whined. "I'm scared and it hurts so bad."

"I'll be as gentle as possible," Roxanne promised. "You ready?" Lexia nodded and she carefully lifted her leg and removed her tennis shoe. With Lexia's ankle in her grasp, she said, "Okay, can you wiggle your toes for me?"

Lexia moved her toes and Roxanne grinned. "Well, I have good news, sweetheart. It isn't broken." She reached into her pocket and handed her some pills. "Take these with some water and you'll be okay in no time."

"What are those?" Morgan asked staring down at her.

"Percocet," Roxanne said with a lowered brow.

"I don't want her taking those."

"Well they will help her feel better," Roxanne responded. "And remember what I said, you aren't in charge of this family. I am." She looked at Grace. "Grace, go get your sister some water." Grace rushed to follow orders.

Morgan's temples throbbed she was so angry with Roxanne. Why was she giving a kid a hard drug? She felt like she was losing control. "This is so wrong!"

"Morgan, chill out. Your sister is hurt and the only thing I want to do is make sure she feels better. What she needs is some rest."

Lexia took the pills and the water and handed the cup back to Grace.

"But that doesn't mean she's not in trouble," Morgan advised. "I told her not to go to the skate park and she disobeyed me. And now look."

Roxanne stood up. "Morgan, are you mentally ill?"

"What?" she glared.

"I just want to make sure because I told you five times in the last two minutes alone that you are not in charge. Yet you continue to operate like you are. Now since you don't know how to talk to me, or treat your family, I want you to go to your room. And don't come out until I call for you." When Morgan was about to leave she said, "Oh, Morgan, give me your car keys too." She extended her hand. "Little girls who don't know how to speak to adults shouldn't be behind the wheel either."

Morgan reached in her pocket and slapped the car keys in her palm before storming upstairs.

I hate that dumb bitch!

CHAPTER SEVEN
JUNE 16TH

Dear Diary,

I feel alone and nobody cares. Every day I come to my room because I'm grounded but my sisters go on without me. Petra is the only one who comes to see me but she spends most of her time in her own head and in her own room.
I hate my life.
I hate my stepmother.
And I hate my sisters too.

Morgan lay on her side with her cell phone in her hand. She missed Trevor and was trying to get in contact with him but since school was out, she hadn't seen him. The last time she laid eyes on him was when she dropped him off at home. He hadn't bothered to call her once since. When she called him again and he didn't answer she tossed her phone on the bed and there was a light knock on her bedroom door. She rolled over and sat up. "Come in." She was hoping it was one of her sisters but it was Roxanne instead. "Morgan, why don't you come down and join us for dinner."

Morgan rolled her eyes and lay back down. "I'm not hungry."

"But we want you to join us, sweetheart."

"I'm on punishment, remember?"

Roxanne walked deeper into the room and laid Morgan's car keys on the dresser beside the bed. Morgan tried desperately to hide her excitement because she didn't like her playing games. Either the car was hers or it wasn't. "You're off punishment," Roxanne proclaimed. "So come eat dinner."

"Are you ordering me to come down or asking?"

She exhaled. "I'm asking. For now."

"Well since you're asking, the answer is no."

Roxanne closed the door. She pulled up a chair that was in the corner of the room and sat beside the bed. "Listen, you little bitch. Let me explain something to you. I wouldn't care if your ass stayed in this bitch until you rotted. As a matter of fact, nothing would bring me greater joy. But your sisters are asking for you to come downstairs which is the only reason I'm up here. If it wasn't for my daughters—"

"They aren't your daughters," Morgan spat, shivering at how she was talking to her.

"They are mine. And if someone tried to take them from me, and that means you too, I wouldn't hesitate to kill them."

Morgan's heart rate increased. She knew Roxanne was a monster but never thought she'd show her evil to her face. "What do you really want with my sisters? And my family?" she asked in a low voice. "Because I won't let you hurt them."

"Nothing but total submission." She giggled. "But you don't need to worry about all of that. Now pick your face up, little bitch, before I really give you something to cry about." Roxanne stood up and switched out of the room, slamming the door behind her.

Before making a move, Morgan took a second to think about her family. This woman would be the death of them but what could she do? Her father told her to leave the matter alone and her sisters thought Roxanne was the second coming.

Trying to clear her mind, Morgan stood up and paced the floor. When she was done she leaned up against the window and looked past the oak tree at the grey house across the street. The Gregory twins were playing with a red ball in their front yard. Both girls were dingy as usual and she never understood why. She always told herself that when she had time she would help clean them up and she was sure they'd be so pretty once she got finished with them.

"Mama," Morgan said aloud, "I don't know what to do. I need your help. Please."

ₗ ₗ ₗ

A month passed and nothing changed. Morgan sat on the edge of her bed with her cell phone in her hand. With everything that was going on, she needed somebody in her corner. A friend who cared about her. She needed Trevor. Although he didn't pick up the phone the last ten times she called, that day she decided to give it a chance again. And to her surprise, he answered on the first ring.

"Hello," he said in a dry tone.

Surprised, she said, "Trevor? Is that you?"

"Yeah."

"Trevor, oh my god. Why haven't you been answering my calls? I've been trying to reach you for weeks."

"What you want, Morgan?" he exhaled.

She sighed. It was obvious what he wanted from her and if she wanted to keep him she would have to say it. "I'm ready, Trevor." She twirled the edge of the white cord with her index finger. "I'm ready to have sex with you. Whenever you are."

"You said that before," he sighed.

"But I never said I'm ready tonight."

Silence.

"So if you really ready when you trying to meet?"

"I can pick you up later on tonight. I don't know where we'll go but I'm sure we can find someplace." She walked over to her window and focused on the big oak tree. "Trevor, if we, you know, are things going to be different with us afterwards? Because I don't want to lose you."

"You know it's not just about sex with me."

"Then what is it about?"

"It's about going to the next level before I go to college. You real pretty, Morgan. And I don't want to leave only for some other dude to have that moment with you. I don't want to lose you and I feel like if we do this we'll stay together forever. You feel me?"

"Yes." She paused. "I think so."

"Good," he said excitedly. "Well let me get dressed." She was about to hang up until he said, "Aye, Morgan?"

"Yes."

"I love you."

"I love you too." She blushed.

"Call me when you on your way."

When she got off the phone with him, she thought more about her sisters. Not only had they grown further apart but now when she entered a room they would stop talking like she was an outsider and it hurt her feelings. Whenever she talked to her father about it he would say, "You're the oldest, Morgan. You should work more to fit in with your sisters instead of fighting with them."

So she stayed alone. She was just about to get up and get dressed when Lexia walked in and said, "Can you braid the front of my hair again?"

Morgan rolled her eyes but she knew she was going to do it anyway. Because at least she would have time with her. "Why don't you ask Roxanne?"

She giggled. "Come on, sis. You know she don't do 'em right."

Morgan took a few minutes to re-braid her hair but that was another thing that angered her about her sisters. She felt used. It was okay for them to ask her to do stuff for them but when the favors were done, they were off kissing Roxanne's ass again. Every day they made it obvious behind the stepmother's back that they needed her. But when Roxanne was home they avoided her like the plague.

When Morgan finished, Lexia rushed out when she heard Roxanne call her name. She exhaled just as Petra was coming into her room. "What you doing?"

"About to go see Trevor." She went over to the dresser to brush her hair. "I had to re-braid the front of Lexia's head first though."

"Oh," she sighed. "I meant to tell you, I don't like him. I never have."

Morgan frowned and put her brush down. "Why you say that? You used to have a crush on him."

"Because you haven't been happy and boyfriends should make you happy. Every time you say his name now, you look sad. What is he doing to you to make you look that way?"

"Don't worry about all that," Morgan said as she walked toward her closet. "You need to be concerned with why you so weird instead of what me and Trevor got going on."

Petra laughed. "You know what your problem is?"

Morgan slammed the door shut and put her hands on her hips. "What is my problem? Because right now it seems like my only issue is you."

"Your problem is that you gave up too easily."

"How did I give up easily? Me and Trevor back together now."

"I'm not talking about Trevor," Petra said. "I'm talking about the sisters."

Morgan shrugged. "Well I'm not thinking about them anymore. If they don't want me in their lives they don't have to have me." She turned around and took off her jeans to slide on another pair. "They can have Roxanne. I don't care."

"That's another thing. You're thinking about Roxanne instead of how to get to them. You know your sisters."

"What are you saying? Because I'm tired of playing games now."

"It's not about you, Morgan. It's about us. If that bitch keeps her nails in the sisters, do you know what will happen? They may die." Morgan didn't seem convinced. "Did you know that Lexia has been popping pain pills ever since Roxanne gave her the one when she twisted her ankle? I think she may be using them every day."

Morgan's jaw dropped and she covered her mouth with her fingertips.

"Well she has. And if you ask me, I think she's getting addicted. Now you have to get them away from her."

"But I don't know how."

"It's really simple. Make them jealous. If you find a way to make them see how it would be if you weren't in their lives, you'll win." Petra walked out of the room.

Morgan knew Petra was on to something. Now the problem was how could she make them envious. She paced around her room before she ended up at her window. When she looked past the oak tree, she saw the Gregory sisters playing with a ball in the front yard again.

Suddenly she had her answer. But setting her plan in motion would entail breaking her date with Trevor. She only hoped he would understand.

👢 👢 👢

For the next week, Morgan essentially adopted the Gregory twins. The first thing she did was bring them into the house and get their hairstyles together. Both of them received perms, trims and nice curled bobs, courtesy of Morgan. When their hair was in order, Morgan asked her father for some money. And since cash flow was never a problem for the Collins family, he gave her five hundred dollars, which she used to buy new clothes for them.

Every day the Gregory twins were at the house and Morgan poured all of her time and attention into making them stars. Before long, the neighborhood boys took notice and the fourteen-year-olds went from nobodies to rock stars and they had Morgan to thank.

Once the girls were to her liking, Morgan officially introduced them to the family. The three of them would enjoy meals at the house and tell inside jokes that only they knew. This drove the Collins sisters, with the exception of Petra, crazy. Petra knew what was going on and she loved it.

Although Roxanne didn't like strangers in the house, she didn't say much about Morgan's new friends. Besides, she was relieved that Morgan wasn't acting like a bitch anymore and was actually out of her room and interacting with everyone else. As long as the strange twins stayed out of her way,

Roxanne could care less about Morgan's pet project. But her sisters felt differently.

A few weeks later, Morgan was in her room with the Gregory twins when Lexia knocked on the door. They were in mid-conversation, which stopped the moment she knocked. Lexia smiled at the twins and focused on her big sister. "Hey, Morgan." She stuffed her hands in her pockets. "You got a sec?"

"What's up?"

"You mind re-braiding the front of my hair again?" she asked rubbing the sections that needed work. "It's messed up again and I don't have an appointment until next week. I don't want to go to the skate park like this."

"Oh, I'm so sorry, Lex," Morgan responded. "But I'm about to curl Cake's hair," she said referring to one of the twins.

"Okay, well what about later?"

"Later we're going to the movies," Morgan continued as if she were sad. "Why don't you ask Roxanne? I'm sure she can hook it up for you. I think she said she knew how to do them smaller for you and everything."

"But I don't like how she does it," Lexia pleaded. "Can you at least do it for me tomorrow?"

"I can't do it then either," she replied shaking her head. "I'm sorry, Lex. Unfortunately, I just don't have a lot of free time on my hands anymore."

Lexia looked at the twins and back at Morgan. "Okay, well thank you anyway." She walked out of the room with her head hung low. Morgan felt slightly guilty but she realized the bigger plan.

She wasn't the only one with a broken heart. Grace and Shaye came to Morgan's room too and as she did with Lexia, she denied their requests also. Morgan distanced herself from her sisters for two more weeks and after awhile her rejection showed up in their moods. Suddenly they weren't interested in shopping sprees with Roxanne, or talk sessions that went on well into the night. They were thinking about their big sister and why she was ignoring them for the twins across the street.

One Saturday afternoon Roxanne came home with two bags full of groceries. The plan was to make pizza with the girls and watch movies, in the hopes of putting them in a better mood. She didn't know what was going on but she felt their disconnection and was certain that Morgan had something to do with it. But the moment she sat the bags down on the dining room table and saw their faces were longer than ever, she was heated. "What's going on?" she asked as she removed a gallon of milk from the bag and placed it on the table. She looked around at the girls again. "Well, is anybody going to talk to me or am I talking to myself?"

"Nothing's wrong," Lexia said shrugging.

"Yeah, we're fine," Grace responded as she stood up to help put away the groceries.

Roxanne, Lexia, Grace and Shaye put all of the food up and when they were done, they made pizzas and put them in the oven. Although they helped with the meal, they still weren't in their usual cheerful moods. Hoping a comedy DVD would help, she put it in the player and they all sat in the living room. Five minutes later, she was the only one laughing. They were quiet and appeared depressed. It was as if they lost their best friend.

Later, Morgan came in with the Gregory twins and they sat in the dining room, eating ice cream and talking about neighborhood cuties. The sisters were more interested in what Morgan and the twins were doing than anything else.

When Roxanne looked harder and saw Morgan smiling a little too wide and heard her laughing a little too loud, she finally got it. Morgan had cut her sisters off and adopted the Gregory twins to make them angry.

Very smart, Roxanne thought. *I didn't consider you a worthy opponent. That was a mistake on my part. But it won't happen again.*

Morgan sat up in bed and stretched her arms toward the ceiling on a sunny Saturday morning. Keeping with her plan to hook up with the Gregorys, she got dressed and did her hair. She was surprised that although it was only 11:00am, she didn't hear the normal chattering downstairs in the house. Although she was still in get-the-sisters-jealous mode, the plan was to stop the charade this weekend. She was sure that once she made herself available to them, they would make themselves available to her. Plus she missed them a lot.

Before leaving, Morgan called the twins. Normally whenever they saw her number, they would pick up the phone right away. But this time when she called she got nothing.

So she decided to call Trevor. Since the Gregory project, she hadn't bothered to call him at all. She picked the phone up on the dresser and dialed his number. It rang once and he answered. "Trevor," she swallowed, "it's me. Morgan. Where have you been?"

"What you talking 'bout?" he asked with an attitude. "I been around, Morgan. And it ain't like you called me."

"I know. I wanted to call you but things have been crazy here."

"Well, I got accepted into Florida University in case you wanted to know. On a football scholarship."

She smiled. Although they weren't talking anymore, she was really happy for him. "I'm so excited for you, Trevor. Let me take you out to celebrate. For lunch maybe?"

"Why? So you can stand me up again? No thanks, I'm good."

She exhaled. "Trevor, I'm sorry. You know Roxanne is here and…well…there's so much stuff going on with my sisters and—"

"They are all you care about." He laughed bitterly. "And now I finally get it."

"Can we start all over, Trevor? I want to prove to you that I can be about you and only you. Please."

"I'll call you and let you know. As busy as things have been for me, I'm not sure I have any more time for you." He hung up.

Morgan took a moment to think about her situation. Revenge had left her boyfriend-less and lonely. This war with Roxanne was too costly.

After she got off the phone, she grabbed her purse and her keys. Since the twins weren't answering, she decided to go across the street to get them. The moment she walked downstairs, she saw Shaye, Grace and Lexia huddled around Roxanne as she sat on the sofa. Hollis was on her left and when he saw his daughter he smiled. "So you finally came out for some air?" he grinned. "Why don't you come over here, baby, and hang out with us? We miss you in this family. You've been keeping so much time with the Gregory girls that you're never around anymore."

For a second Morgan thought about throwing in the towel because she wanted nothing more than to be with her family. But when she saw the sly grin on Roxanne's face and how her sisters had their noses turned up in her direction she frowned. "Naw, I got something to do." She moved toward the door. "Maybe later though."

"Well make sure you're back in time for dinner," Roxanne said. "The summer break is almost over and school starts next month. And I need to make sure you're on the right schedule. So tonight I want you in early. Okay?"

"Yeah, whatever," Morgan said as she reached for the door.

"Morgan!" Hollis yelled. "Where are your manners?"

She exhaled. "Sorry, daddy," she said dryly. She looked at Roxanne. "I'll be in early."

Morgan knew the curfew was another way for Roxanne to control her but what could she do? She was willing to stay grounded just as long as she and her sisters were back together when it was all said and done.

When she walked outside she saw Petra standing on the step flicking matches onto the front porch. "You know daddy inside on the living room couch, right?"

"Yeah."

"Yeah, well if he sees you you're grounded."

"In my world I'm always grounded." She paused. "Besides, you and I both know I get to do whatever I want. That's one of the benefits of being crazy, remember?"

Morgan sighed as she shook her head. "If you say so."

Petra looked at the door and then back at Morgan. "Did you see that corny shit in the house? They huddled on the couch like they're about to have an orgy or something."

"I know," Morgan sighed as she looked at the Gregory house. "I can't believe how easy it is for them to accept her as our mother. It's like ma was never here."

"Don't say that. They miss mama," Petra said under her breath. "We all do. Maybe for now any set of warm titties will do." Morgan nodded and walked past Petra. "Where you going?"

"About to walk to the Gregory twins' house."

"I'm going with you." Petra stuffed the matches in her pocket and bounced behind her. "I don't have anything else to do."

They walked across the street and knocked on the door. Within a few seconds, Mrs. Gregory flung the door open. A cigarette dangled between her fingertips and her other hand clutched a glass of scotch. "What you want?" she asked, narrowing her eyes at Morgan.

Morgan was taken aback by her attitude. If anything, she should feel grateful that she elevated her daughters from the off brand status they were accustomed to. "I'm here for the twins. Are they home?"

"Let me tell you something, bitch," she said pointing the cigarette at her. "I want you to stay the fuck from around here. The fuck from around my kids. I know who you really are, Morgan." She looked her up and down. "And I don't like it one bit."

"What are you trying to say?" Morgan asked, totally confused.

"You're a dyke with a taste for my girls," she said as a clump of ashes floated to the ground. "Now get the fuck off of my steps so I can wash them!" she yelled before taking another puff.

Morgan backed up, turned around and rushed down the stairs. She was angry with herself for allowing tears to fall from her eyes. What was she talking about? The last thing she wanted was to sleep with the Gregory twins. She wasn't even gay.

"Instead of cleaning your steps, you need to clean your fucking kids," Petra yelled at her. "Before my sister took care of 'em, they smelled like the seat of your old ass panties, you washed up ass bitch!"

Mrs. Gregory gasped and slammed the door in their faces.

Petra rushed over to Morgan who was hyperventilating. "You okay, sis?"

"I don't know what she's talking about," Morgan admitted, wiping the tears from her eyes. "I would never do anything like that to them. I mean, where did she get that from?"

"You know where she got it from."

Just as Petra said those words, Roxanne came out of their house with a lit cigarette. Morgan and Petra didn't even know she smoked. Roxanne was looking directly at Morgan with a grin on her face. She took one more puff, blew a cloud of smoke into the air and walked back into the house.

THE MEANEST OF THEM ALL

CHAPTER EIGHT
AUGUST 5TH

Dear Diary,
I haven't spoken to my sisters in awhile. I'm not sure what Roxanne is saying to them but whatever it is, it's working. These days the only person I have in my corner is Petra and as bad as I've been feeling, I'm grateful.
I miss mama more than anything.

August 3rd

When Morgan rolled over in bed, she heard Lexia yelling, "Petra burned my hair!" She shook her head and slipped on her sweatpants. If there was one person who didn't change in the Collins home, Petra was it. With both feet planted on the floor, she looked at the oak tree. She sighed as she thought about her life. With her family ignoring her for whatever reason and her boyfriend avoiding her calls, she was lonely.

She needed an escape, but she didn't want to give Roxanne the satisfaction of seeing her drive the car she bought for her. All she wanted was to get out of the house and away from the woman who she despised. Then she'd be away from the negativity. Away from the games. But all of that was just a dream.

She decided to walk up the block but one block turned into two and then three and after walking for an hour, she realized it was time to go back home. Not trying to rush, she decided to take the scenic route through a park, which had a bike trail. She was gone for two hours and when she opened the door, she was surprised that it was quiet. Too quiet.

Normally she would go directly to her room but curiosity got the best of her. Where was everyone? She walked to Lexia's room and she wasn't there. She went to Grace's room and she wasn't there either. But when she went to Shaye and then Petra's room she got worried. Petra never left the house unless she was with her. Concerned, she walked to her father's room and he was gone. And so was Roxanne.

"What's going on?" she said to herself suspiciously. When she searched the entire house again and couldn't find anyone, she figured there was one more place to go. The basement. She knew it was fruitless because no one ever went down there but she decided to give it a try anyway.

So she walked downstairs and opened the door leading to the basement. Slowly she trailed down the stairs and paused when she heard moaning. She pushed herself further down and her heart stopped when she saw Roxanne sitting on a large chair. On the floor was Trevor, standing on his knees with his hands on her thighs, giving her oral sex.

Morgan thought she was seeing things at first. How could her boyfriend and her stepmother be having sex in their house? When did they have a chance to hook up? She'd never even seen them talk. But when she blinked several times and he was still lapping Roxanne's clit she knew it was real.

When Roxanne took a moment to open her eyes she saw her grief stricken stepdaughter. Although Roxanne spotted her immediately, Trevor was too deep in her bush to notice that they were caught. To make things worse, Roxanne winked and that's what set her off.

Devastated, Morgan grabbed a baseball bat sitting by the steps and charged toward Trevor's back. When Roxanne tapped him on the shoulder to alert him, he turned around and saw his angry girl-friend. He sure as hell knew she was there now. Trevor tried to jump out of the way but Morgan swung left and right until she landed on the back of his head and shoulders.

"Stop! Stop!" Trevor yelled hopping around the basement. "What are you doing, baby?"

"Get out of my house!" Morgan screamed as tears rolled down her face. "I hate you and I never want to see you again! You dirty dick ass nigga! How could you? In my house!"

"I'm sorry, Morgan," he said with pleading eyes as she pinned him up in a corner. The bat was hanging over him and she contemplated busting his head wide open. "I was coming over here to sur-prise you and—"

"You fucked my stepmother," she yelled, completing his sentence. When she looked at him she finally got what Petra meant when she said she didn't like him. He wasn't worth it. She wasted all of her time on a loser but at least she could say one thing—she didn't give him her virginity. She dropped the bat. "Get out of my house, Trevor," she exhaled. "And don't come back here."

With his shoulders slouched, he sighed and said, "Okay. But I still love you."

When he moved to touch her she reached down and picked up the bat again. "Don't make me regret leaving you alive, Trevor. You don't know the things me and my family is capable of. Now leave." Morgan hated hearing those words coming out of his mouth and would not tolerate hearing them again. It all sounded so stupid now. How could he love her when he had done the ultimate? It was impossible!

When he trudged up the steps and she heard the front door close, she turned around and focused her anger on Roxanne. She was about to hit her when Roxanne said, "I would rip your shoulders off your body, little girl." Her voice was calm and menacing. "Because although I don't know what your family is capable of, you have no idea the things that I've done either."

Morgan stopped in her tracks, looked at the monster and dropped the bat again. The moment it clanked against the floor, Morgan's body convulsed and she broke out into tears. "How did you get everybody out of the house, so you could fuck my boyfriend? Huh, whore?"

"I told them that the house was being fumigated," she said slyly. "For rats."

"And yet the biggest rat is right here," Morgan said wiping her tears away.

"Touché," Roxanne responded.

"I'm going to tell my daddy," she promised. "I'm going to tell him that you're a pedophile who had sex with a child. What do you think he'll do then, Roxanne?" She paused. "I'll tell you what he'll do. He'll throw your funky ass out on the streets where you belong."

"You will do no such thing," she said fixing her skirt.

"Yes I will! If you think I won't you don't know me at all!"

Roxanne laughed. "If you're thinking about telling my husband anything I will ruin you. Besides, I did you a favor. Your little boy toy and me have been fucking for the past month. Haven't you wondered why he wasn't answering your calls? I own him. Just like I own your father." She giggled. "You started the war, Morgan. I'm just finishing it."

Morgan was so angry that she felt like she could rip her eyes out but another look at Roxanne told her that she would have her hands full. "I'm still going to tell. I don't care what you say."

Roxanne wiped the smile off her face. "If you do that…if you tell your father anything, I will hurt you more than you can imagine."

"How?"

"By harming what you love most of all. One of your sisters." She walked up to Morgan. "Do yourself a favor, little girl. Let it go." She walked upstairs and out of sight.

Once again, Morgan Collins couldn't sleep. Day in and day out, she obsessed over Roxanne. She wanted to tell her sisters what happened with her boyfriend but Roxanne threatened her daily. So without telling them why, for the next few days Morgan tried to warn her sisters to stay away from Roxanne. The only one who heeded her warning was the same one who listened to her anyway, Petra.

Why wouldn't the sisters believe her? She couldn't wrap her mind around it. She still remembered the conversation she had with Lexia who was so pro Roxanne, she was still calling the woman her mother. "You're just jealous, Morgan! And we aren't listening to you anymore," Lexia asserted. "Why don't you go tell the Gregory twins since they're your new sisters and you like them more than us?"

As the days went by, she was resigned to the fact that nothing she said would work. Besides, she felt foolish crying wolf when there was no sign of danger in sight. Roxanne still hadn't hurt anybody despite her threat in the basement. At least she had that to be grateful for.

Morgan was sitting in her room looking out of her window. She thought about telling her father everything. But every time he came home, Roxanne would take him into the bedroom, sex him down and make him repeat how much she was in control.

She's right, Morgan thought to herself. *She really is in control of everything. Even me and my life.*

Lying in bed, she rolled over and looked out of the window. The leaves on the oak tree blew in the wind. Large tears rolled down her cheeks until suddenly she saw Lexia climbing the tree. Lately she had been doing that a lot despite Morgan telling her not to in the past. The last time Morgan threatened her about climbing the tree, Lexia told the stepmother who scolded Morgan for trying to run the family again. As she did before, she took the car keys and grounded her for a week. She said the reason for the punishment was that Morgan needed to learn her position as a child.

Lexia was almost to the top of the tree when Morgan noticed something. The largest branch was shaking more than usual. She hopped up and squinted to try to identify the reason. That's when she saw it. There was a crack in the branch. She rushed to the window to warn Lexia but it was too late. Lexia Collins went crashing down twenty-five feet to the ground.

⟨ ⟨ ⟨

The bowl of chicken noodle soup sitting on the tray with crackers shook as Morgan walked up the stairs carefully. When she got to Lexia's door she sat it down and knocked softly. Lexia didn't answer but Morgan knew she was inside. How could she leave when she couldn't walk? It had been a week since the accident and Lexia hadn't said a word to anyone so Morgan decided to go to her.

When she still didn't answer she opened the door, lifted the tray and walked inside. Lexia sat across the room in a wheelchair with her back faced Morgan's direction. She was looking out of the window, at the oak tree in the backyard. The same one that left her paralyzed from the waist down.

Morgan put the soup and crackers on the dresser and walked behind the wheelchair. The room smelled stale and borderline offensive. "It's time to eat, Lexia," Morgan whispered. She turned the wheelchair around so that she was facing her and pushed it toward the bed. "You been starving yourself too long. That stops today."

Lexia sighed and dropped her head. She couldn't fight with her when she couldn't move.

Morgan picked up the food from the dresser, walked over to the bed and sat it down. She also took a seat and looked over her sister. Her heart ached because Lexia was the last person she wanted to see paralyzed. What was an adventurer without her legs?

Morgan dipped the spoon into the soup and said, "Open your mouth."

Lexia obeyed.

Morgan dipped spoon after spoon into the food, depositing granules of crackers in her mouth in between, until the meal was gone. When she was done she wiped the corners of her sister's mouth. "Was it good? Shaye made it especially for you. Put fresh vegatables inside and everything."

Lexia lowered her head and tears rolled out of her eyes.

"Please don't cry anymore, Lexia. I'm begging you."

"I ain't got no body," Lexia mumbled. "I ain't got nothing."

Since Lexia was paralyzed, Roxanne, her prized stepmother, abandoned her. Roxanne couldn't stand to look at the imp because it was bad enough that she had to hear her husband cry about his child's accident. In Roxanne's opinion, it would have been better if she had died. That way, she wouldn't be forced to see Hollis carrying her up and down the steps as his tears fell on her face.

"Have they been here?" Morgan asked. "The sisters?"

Lexia cried harder before covering her mouth to stop her lips from trembling. "No," she said shaking her head. "Not anymore."

In the beginning, the sisters would come by once a day but since Lexia wouldn't talk to them, things got weird so they decided to leave her to her misery. They loved her. They truly did. But it was hard seeing their adventurous sister confined to a wheelchair so they decided to pretend as if she wasn't there.

"Just kill me," Lexia begged as Morgan wiped her mouth again. "I don't want to live anymore."

Morgan's heart pounded so hard in her chest upon hearing those words that the napkin dropped out of her hand. "What are you talking about?" she asked looking her up and down. "Huh?" she demanded. She pointed a finger in her face. "Never speak like that again, Lexia."

"But I'm serious, Morgan," she continued as tears trailed down her face. "Please kill me. I'm begging you." She wiped her face with the back of her hand. "Or else I'm gonna do it myself. I just have to figure out how."

Morgan gripped her by her shoulders. "How could you give up on life without even trying? You still got the use of your arms, don't you? Ain't that good for something?" She paused. "If I were you I wouldn't let Roxanne think she got the best of me by talking like that."

"You think Roxanne had something to do with my fall?"

"Lexy, come on, I told you she's out for me. She already threatened to hurt who I love." Morgan explained.

Lexia sat with her thoughts before becoming overwhelmed with sorrow. "But you don't understand," she cried harder. "If I can't walk, skate or climb I don't want to live."

Morgan leaned back. She knew her sister was serious and made a decision that she could not leave her alone. She would not allow Lexia to fall astray. At least not without a fight. She had to do something. For starters, she made a decision to move into her room whether she wanted her to or not. "Lexia, we are going to beat this. You are about to go through the hardest thing you ever experienced in your life. But I promise you, if you trust me, at the end of it all you will walk again."

"But the doctor said I would never walk."

"And you believe him? Or do you believe me?"

For the next week, before working with Lexia, Morgan read up on everything she could find about physical therapy and paralysis. When she had all of the knowledge she could hold, she created a physical therapy plan for Lexia. Morgan started with stretching her limbs so that she would remain limber. With each passing day, Lexia was able to stretch more.

Slowly Morgan started incorporating physical therapy exercises into the routine. For the first few weeks, there was no movement in her lower legs and Lexia grew hopeless although Morgan remained optimistic. Despite Lexia's growing frustrations, she kept trying to move her toes.

Before long, Morgan became Lexia's shadow. She accompanied her on the outside physical therapy appointments. She updated the therapist on what Lexia was able to do and the doctor was always impressed with her progress. Hollis would come every now and again but Roxanne was sexing him so well that he didn't have the energy to keep up with the morning appointments. Neither Morgan nor Lexia cared because they were focused on one thing, getting her to walk again.

When another month passed and Morgan asked Lexia to move whatever she could on her body, like she did each morning, her jaw dropped when Lexia wiggled a toe.

"Oh my god, Lexia," Morgan yelled jumping up and down. "You did it! You fucking did it!" Morgan was so excited that she took to jumping around the room, causing the entire house to rock.

Upon hearing the noise upstairs the Collins sisters, with Roxanne in tow, rushed up to see what was going on. When Grace opened the door, they saw Morgan standing in the middle of the room with a half smile on her face while Lexia's arms were folded over her chest.

"What's so funny?" Grace asked excitedly, eager to smile too.

"Nothing," Lexia said rolling her eyes.

"She's right. Lexia was just laughing at something I said that's all. You would not have gotten the joke." Ironically, both Lexia and Morgan acted as if nothing was going on. They made a silent agreement in that moment to keep the small victory to themselves.

With her newfound movement, Lexia and Morgan worked relentlessly both day and night for the next few months. The stale odor in Lexia's room grew thicker because they never left. Even though school was back in session, they decided to be home schooled, which Lexia loved. She hated the thought of wheeling herself into school everyday. The strides that the sisters made were so extraordinary that they even stopped going to outside physical therapy sessions. It was apparent that the therapists couldn't do anything for Lexia that Morgan couldn't. As months went by, so did the seasons. They didn't speak to the family much and outside of talking to Petra every now and again, they pretty much avoided everyone else. They were obsessed with her getting well.

It wasn't until Christmas day that Morgan and Lexia decided to show the family how far they'd gotten. Everyone was gathered downstairs by the Christmas tree when Morgan walked down to greet them. Her red hair had grown longer and it was messy as usual. "Excuse me," Morgan said under her breath. "Can I have your attention?"

Everyone, including Petra who was drinking hot chocolate at the dining room table, gave her their attention. "I would like five minutes of your time. Lexia has something to show you."

Everyone in the family was excited that Morgan was speaking to them, except Roxanne. She had grown used to not seeing her.

"Sure, honey," Hollis said. "Can I help you with anything?"

"If you can help me bring Lexia down that would be great."

Hollis sat his spiked eggnog down and rushed up the stairs to Lexia's room. He lifted her out of the chair and Morgan grabbed the wheelchair. Petra held the door open and the three of them walked back to the living room. Once they were downstairs, Morgan sat the chair in front of the tree and Hollis sat his daughter down in it. Morgan and Lexia smiled at one another, knowing the plan.

When the family was assembled around them, Morgan looked at them all and said, "Our family has been through a lot over the last year. With losing mama and Lexia falling." She cleared her throat. "Well, things have been hard and I understand my part in all of this." She looked her sisters in the eyes. "And I want to say that I'm sorry. For everything."

"Honey, don't worry about it," Hollis said as he heard his daughter's pleas. "You meant well and everybody handles death differently. You handled it the best way you could."

"Let her apologize," Roxanne interrupted him. "She knows what she's been doing and she knows what she's sorry for. If you ask me, this apology is long overdue."

"That's why nobody's asking you, you a stupid bitch," Petra yelled. "You always got something smart—"

"Petra!" Hollis screamed.

"Don't do that," Morgan said as she raised her hand at her sister and looked at her daddy to calm him down too. "It's okay, Petra. She's right. I need to apologize." She swallowed and looked down at Lexia who was smiling up at her. "Plus it's not about me. This is about Lexia. She and I have isolated ourselves for months and I didn't take into consideration your feelings while doing that." She squeezed Lexia's hand. "But there is a reason we've been hiding upstairs." She looked at Lexia. "Me and Lexy both want to show you something. Go ahead, Lexy."

Lexia took a deep breath and gripped the arms of the wheelchair tightly. It rattled under her weight. Slowly she eased up and Hollis jumped out of his seat when he saw her buckle. "Daddy, no," Morgan said with her hand extended. "Let her do this. She'll be okay. Trust me."

Lexia continued to push on the arms of the chair until she was on her feet. Everyone but Roxanne sat on the edge of their seats as if they were watching a horror movie. Would Lexia plummet to the ground? No she would not. Instead, she took her first step followed by her next. And before long, she was walking shakily toward her father. His eyes widened as he saw his child move toward him after believing, as the doctors said, that she would never walk again. Lexia didn't stop until she was in her father's arms.

Once she was in front of him, Hollis gripped her tightly and sobbed. She took a moment to rest as she allowed his strength to keep her off her feet. "Oh my God! Baby, you did it! You walked."

"It was Morgan," Lexia sobbed. "She wouldn't give up on me, daddy."

The sisters were stunned as they saw what the power of love could do. They knew their oldest sister was the best and was always there for them but she outdid herself this time. They all looked upon her as if she was a God. All but one. Roxanne Collins glared at the elated Morgan.

"I'm so happy for you," Grace said as she hugged Lexia while she was in her father's arms. "I really got my sister back now."

Even Shaye took to hugging Lexia and Hollis before both of them turned their attention to Morgan. But instead of drowning in the love and admiration they were showing her, Morgan walked upstairs to be alone.

Roxanne looked at Morgan as she ascended the stairs with daggers in her eyes. Always seeing things as a competition, she tried to think of how she could come behind Morgan now? Had she known she was in the room playing God, she would've framed her for something she didn't do and grounded her for months. At the very least, she would've separated them and prevented them from spending so much time alone. So what Lexia would never walk? That was not of her concern.

Morgan was in her own room, sitting Indian style on the carpet, playing solitaire with a deck of cards. She smiled as she heard the cheers for Lexia's recovery downstairs. The family had many Christmas days but this was the best of them all.

When her bedroom door opened she was looking at Petra.

"Why aren't you downstairs?" Morgan asked seriously. "You should be with the family, Petra. It's Christmas and I don't want people to think I'm trying to put you against anyone."

"I'm not down there because I'm spending time with you," she responded. "I'm proud of you, big sis. You showed that bitch. You should've saw her face."

"Whoa," Morgan giggled. "Since when did you get all sentimental?"

"I'm serious. I knew you could do anything but I never saw this coming." She paused. "But you know Roxanne is going to really be mad now, right?"

She rolled her eyes. "Yeah, well what's new?"

Petra laughed, walked over to Morgan's closet and grabbed the monopoly game. "You trying to lose?"

Morgan grinned. "When are you going to learn? I can't lose."

CHAPTER NINE
JANUARY 3RD

Dear Diary,

Since Lexia started walking, I reunited with my sisters and we spend a lot of time together. It reminds me of the good old days when we would talk, laugh and even fight. It's as if mama is alive and sometimes I sit on the steps and wait for her to come down to make us breakfast. But she never does.

Although she's gone, I'm happy.

Too happy.

Which is how I know it won't last.

January 14th

The Collins sisters' constant giggling within the house irritated Roxanne as she sat on the edge of the bed while Hollis got dressed for work. "I don't think you're giving this enough attention, Hollis, and I would appreciate your support. You are my fucking husband!"

"And you have it," he sighed as he put his tie around his neck. "But from what you're telling me, I don't see a problem."

"Well I do!" she yelled. "She's at it again. Morgan! With her young ass mind games. Don't you see it? The others don't even talk to me anymore."

"Honey, you are looking too much into things. Morgan is just a child. She isn't formulating this grand plan to overthrow you. All she wants to do is be with her sisters and considering all of the animosity that has been going on in my household, I welcome it. Focus on the miracle this family has been given, courtesy of Morgan. The child should be rewarded."

If she was hot before, she was steaming mad now. "Are you saying that I'm not grateful about Lexia's recovery?" Roxanne asked placing her hand over her heart.

"Of course I'm not saying that. I know that you're happy like I am that Lexia is walking again. I just think that this moment belongs to my daughters and you should allow them to enjoy it. When things settle down at work we'll take a vacation."

When she heard them walking up the stairs, probably to Morgan's room, she stopped talking for a while. She didn't want Morgan to know that she considered her a threat. When she didn't hear footsteps anymore she pouted and crossed her arms over her chest. "So now they are your daughters?" she said ignoring the vacation comment. "I thought you said they were our children."

"Let me be clear on something, Roxanne, they've always been my daughters," he said firmly. "I have allowed you to enjoy them because I understand you can't have any children." He placed his watch on and sat on the edge of the bed next to her. "Now I'm sorry to be so serious with you but if you can't handle my family, maybe you should leave."

"Are you asking for a divorce, Hollis?"

"No. I want to remain married to you but things are going to change, Roxanne. I've been out of touch with my family too long now." He sighed. "And I've regretted a lot of things since Annie died. But after witnessing what Morgan did for Lexia…I just…I just realize that what I thought my family needed, they didn't. What they needed was a father to be there for them in their time of need and I failed. But I'm not failing anymore."

"What does that mean?" she yelled. She frowned and walked across the room. "Because it sounds like you do want me to leave. And that you're blaming me for everything. I didn't cut the branch on the tree, you know."

"Roxanne, I've already said I don't want you to go. But what I do want you to do is back the fuck off." He kissed her on the forehead and walked out the door.

Roxanne was inside of Morgan's room and she was on a rampage. On her hands and knees, she was peeking under her bed searching for what she wanted. When she didn't see it, she raised the mattress and looked under it too. Still no luck.

Annoyed, she walked over to the dresser again. She had already been through the drawers and was unsuccessful but she figured she must've missed something. I mean, how many places in a teenager's room were there to hide a diary.

Frustrated, she focused on the picture of Annie. She crossed her arms over her chest and frowned at it. "You spoiled them too much," she said. "Thanks a lot, bitch!" She sighed. "But it's okay because do or die, I will get them in line." When she observed the silver frame, she thought it was shaped oddly. So she lifted it and flipped it over to survey it. She realized the back was awfully large and when she saw a latch she gave it a nudge and Morgan's brown leather journal fell out. She smiled. "Ah, ha! I got you now!"

Roxanne prepared a huge meal of fried chicken, spinach, mashed potatoes and cornbread. The Collins, still giddy over Lexia's recovery, ate at the table and enjoyed the meal as a family as they chatted amongst themselves. Even Morgan and Petra were present, which was unlike them. Since Roxanne entered the family, Morgan and Petra would eat their meals in the living room or in their bedrooms to avoid her. Basically wherever Roxanne was, they were not. Hollis stayed with the girls for fifteen minutes before he was off to work.

When everyone was done Roxanne stood up from the table and addressed the group. Morgan and Petra looked at each other, tiring already of her speech. This time Lexia also looked over at Morgan and smiled. She was no longer a fool for Roxanne and as far as she was concerned, she would never be again.

"I wanted to personally say that I am pleased to be a part of this family. I know I said it before but I'll say it again because it comes from my heart." She put her hand on her chest. "It has been over a year and not only have I grown to love this family, but I also feel like I'm really your mother."

Morgan and Petra looked at each other again in annoyance. That bitch would never be their mother but to keep the peace, they would let her have it. Although they both fell back on taunting Roxanne, they didn't want to take too much of her at one time either.

"What's up, Roxanne?" Lexia asked. "You getting serious on us? Because I was kind of hoping that we could just keep things light from here on out."

"I'm afraid I have to get a little serious now, honey," she said looking at her before focusing on Morgan. She took a deep breath like she was preparing to do the hardest thing she ever had to do in her life. "Since I got here, Morgan has made it known that she doesn't like me. I'm sorry...she along with Petra have made it known through their actions and how they talk to me."

"Why you doing this right now?" Grace asked loudly. "Like Lexia said, we don't want to fight with each other anymore."

"First off, I'm not fighting with Morgan. She is a child. And I'm making this speech because it must be done," she replied. "I didn't even tell your father because I wanted to work it out with you girls. At first I thought it was me who was causing all of the problems. I felt maybe I was too pushy and tried too hard to fit in."

"You did," Petra announced. "You always try too hard just like you're doing right now. Despite everyone saying they don't want to fight anymore."

"I'm not surprised that you feel that way. You've always stood with Morgan. You even tried to kill me after learning that I was allergic to ant bites. Let's see how you feel when I finish reading this." She pulled out three folded pieces of paper from her pocket.

Morgan immediately sat up straight when she recognized the paper. They belonged to her diary. She pushed back in the chair, stood up and moved toward her but Roxanne rushed to the other side of the table. "Give me the pages of my diary, Roxanne! I know you stole them!"

"Don't worry, Morgan. You can have them back *after* I read what I want to your sisters of course." She grinned. "Unless you have something to hide from them. Do you?"

"It's not about hiding anything. I just don't want you reading my personal shit!"

Roxanne laughed. "Well, sit down, little girl. This won't take too long. And if your sisterhood bond is as tight as you all have made it out to be, you don't have anything to worry about, do you?"

Morgan flopped down in the chair after realizing her worst nightmare was coming true. Right before her eyes.

Roxanne cleared her throat and focused on the first paper. "This passage was done on March 3rd. I'll read only a portion because I'm going to come back to this same sheet later." She cleared her throat. *"Dear Diary, I am writing this entry days late. I couldn't write earlier because so much happened. But I'll try to remember my feelings as best as I can.*

"Let me start by saying I hate Petra. I hate that she's weird. I hate that she's ugly and I hate that she reminds me every day about why I dislike her more than my other sisters. I'm afraid that just

by hanging around her I will get the illness she has. And that I will be like her and mama."

Morgan looked at Petra who was staring down into her lap. Tears welled in the corners of her eyes as she listened to Morgan's hurtful words.

"Can you please stop," Morgan whispered. "I'm begging you. All I want to do is be happy with my family. I'm not even fighting with you anymore. They are all I have left!"

"Why should I stop?" Roxanne grinned. "There's so much more to say." She focused on the diary entries again. *"Dear Diary, if I have to eat another one of Shaye's cookies I think I'm going to puke. I'm tired of being force fed her food when I don't want it just because her precious feelings will be hurt. Every day I pray that both she and Petra go back to a crazy home. Maybe then they will leave me alone."*

Huge tears rolled down Shaye's cheeks and Grace rubbed her shoulder while throwing Morgan evil looks. This was turning out to be the worst day of Morgan's life.

Roxanne, enjoying the change of mood, refocused on the pages again. *"Dear Diary, Grace is such a boy. All she does is fight and hang out with her best friend. I'm starting to wonder if there isn't another reason she's so close to her. Like maybe*

she's gay or something. I hope that's not true be-
cause it will be hard to love her if she is that way.
Isn't that against the bible or something?"

Grace stopped rubbing Shaye and her hand
dropped. She looked as if she wanted to come
across the table at her sister. "I'm not gay," she lied
through clenched teeth.

"I know," Morgan whispered. "But even if
you were I'd still love you."

"But I'm not gay!" Grace slammed her fist into the table.

"Calm down," Roxanne said although she was
smiling harder now. She found it so easy to break a
bond they all claimed was solid. "Anyway I'm not
done just yet." She looked down at the sheets.
"Dear Diary, Lexia can't walk. She fell off a tree
and is partially paralyzed from the waist down.
Every day I feed her. Every day I wash her body
and every day I try to help her move. And I hate her
for it. I warned her to stay out of the tree and she
didn't listen. I bet she wishes she did now."

Lexia was so angry she was trembling like a
volcano about to erupt.

Roxanne tossed the sheets of paper over to
Morgan who folded them up and stuffed them into
her pocket. As if doing so would erase everything
that was said.

"Now I know you all are upset but it was important that you know who you're dealing with," Roxanne continued. "She may be blood but she doesn't love you like I do. She doesn't even care about your feelings. How could she write things like that if she did?"

"Why was it important?" Morgan asked as she looked up at her. "Why was it so important that you tear me away from my family? Who hated you that much that you would come in our home and pour it on me?"

"Nobody hated me," Roxanne said in a low voice. Her lips tightened and it was obvious that she was trying to hold back. "I learned how to hate only after coming here and witnessing what you do to your family. You're the evil one, Morgan, and I'll prove it with this next entry."

"*Dear Diary, I am to blame for mama's death. She reached for me as the fire covered her body and I did nothing. All I had to do was pull her out of the car before it blew up and I couldn't do it. I was too scared. I'm praying that my sisters never find out because I know they'll hate me forever.*"

At first the sisters were hurt but now they were infuriated. As Morgan looked around the table and saw their glares, knowing that she was to blame, her stomach buckled. She leapt up from the table and rushed toward the front door before running into the night.

ᛚ ᛚ ᛚ

Petra was holding the rest of Morgan's diary in her hand as she looked at Grace, Lexia and Shaye. They were weeping hysterically while wondering what she wanted. Morgan's diary entries devastated them. After Roxanne ripped the happiness out of their hearts, she left out to celebrate although she claimed she needed to catch some air.

"Morgan hurt my feelings today," Petra said, "a lot." She swallowed. "And I know she hurt your feelings too. But—"

"We not trying to hear that shit no more, Petra," Grace yelled. "For the past year you been so far up Morgan's ass I thought we'd never find you again. And now you wanna talk to us about the shit she wrote about us in her diary? She talked about you too you know? Don't you have any self-respect?"

"Yeah, Petra, you going too far now with this defense shit," Lexia said while holding onto a cane. She needed it whenever she stood up for long periods. "She said she hated having to help me learn to walk again. If she felt that way why did she even do it?"

"If that's how ya'll really feel, and if ya'll can say that nobody here has ever written a bad thing about another one of us please go upstairs right now and bring me your diaries." She paused and looked at them. "And if you don't I'll just steal them later because I know it's not true." Nobody budged. "That's exactly what I thought," she said shaking her head. "Morgan fucked up but she's still our big sister. She's done a lot for us and deserves a little more credit than that."

"I don't know," Grace admitted. "This time she went way too far."

"I hear you. I really do." She paused. "But Roxanne didn't read you everything in Morgan's diary." She opened the diary and looked at Shaye. "This is what she wrote about you after what Roxanne read to us today at dinner." She focused on the open book. *"Dear Diary, I am so proud of Shaye. Every time I look at her, I'm amazed at her strength. Despite not being what the world deems smart, she proves them wrong every time. Her cooking is amazing and her vanilla cupcakes are my favorite. I can only hope to be one inch the cook she is when I grow up and have a family of my own."*

Petra looked over at Shaye who was smiling brightly.

"This is about you, Grace," Petra said.

"I don't want to hear it."

"Oh, so you can hear what Roxanne's hating ass read about you but you can't hear me out?" She placed her hands on her hips. "How original."

"Go 'head," Grace said with an attitude.

Petra flipped to the passage referring to Grace. *"Dear Diary, today Grace came in with a black eye and although I yelled at her about doing better in school, when she left I cried. Grace doesn't fight because she likes it. She fights to protect those who can't defend themselves and I find that honorable. She's so brave. Maybe if I was as brave as she is I could've saved mama from the car fire. That makes her the strongest person I know."* Petra looked at Grace who had shame spread all over her face.

"Wow," Grace said. "I thought I got on her nerves all of the time. I never knew…"

"You didn't know because Roxanne didn't want us to," Lexia said before looking at Petra. "Read what you want me to hear about myself."

Petra located the passage. *"Dear Diary, today Lexia walked for the first time and I was inspired.*

When I first told her she could do it, I didn't believe it and I hated myself for doubting her. The truth is if she failed, I knew it would be my fault and I wasn't sure I could deal with another family shame. But Lexia never gave up. She believed in me and that made me believe in her too. She's a real live hero and I love her so much." Petra closed the book. "That's our real sister." She paused. "I don't know what happened on the day mama was killed but we all know she has always been afraid of fire." She looked at the floor. "Even I did, which is why I used it against her sometimes when I burned hair. But she loves us and she made a few angry entries, probably when we weren't speaking to her. Who knows? But it doesn't mean she's evil."

"What did she say about you?" Grace asked.

Petra opened the book again and cleared her throat. *"Dear Diary, today Petra spent Christmas with me and I finally understand who she is. She's not some monster. I think she portrays herself as one so that people can't see her heart. But through everything I was going through with the stepmother, she always stood by my side. She kept me strong and I will never forget it. She's my sister and she loves me even if sometimes she has a weird way of showing it."* She closed the book. "There's more but I'm keeping those things to myself."

Grace lowered her head. "This bitch Roxanne has been trying to tear us apart for a long time."

"Yeah, and we let her," Lexia added.

"How didn't I see this coming?" Grace said as she shook her head. "I take up for everybody on the street but my own sister was being fucked with in our own house."

"You didn't see it coming because you wanted what we all did," Lexia said. "A mother."

They heard the door opening upstairs. "Girls, I'm back," Roxanne sang. "Where is everyone?"

"What should we do?" Lexia said leaning in to her sisters.

Grace grabbed a bat. "I don't know about ya'll but I'm about to beat this bitch's ass. And I suggest everybody who don't want to catch a charge stand the fuck back." She moved toward the step. "We're down here," Grace said in a sweet tone.

Instead of standing back all of the girls moved closer to the stairwell, each grabbing what they could as a weapon. The moment Roxanne walked downstairs and Grace could reach her ankle, she pulled it, causing her to tumble down the rest of the stairs. When she was lying on the floor moaning Grace cracked her knees with the bat before dropping it on the floor to straddle her. Once on top, she delivered blow after violent blow until her face was bloody red.

Petra couldn't take it anymore because she was excited about getting some blows in too. So she tapped Grace on the shoulder and she moved out of her way. Once she was up, Petra got on the floor and punched her as many times as she could until Roxanne's lip cracked open. She struck her for everything she did to their family and to Morgan. Then she hit her with a wooden slab lying against the wall, which slit the corner of her eye that was now oozing blood.

Roxanne was too dazed and confused to fight back so everyone was getting the better of her. Right before she passed out, Shaye stood over top of her and kicked her in the head.

🥾 🥾 🥾

Hollis was looking at Roxanne who lay on her side in the bed with a balled up piece of tissue in her palm. She was threatening to do the ultimate: tell the cops what his daughters had done to her.

"Can you at least tell me what happened, Roxanne?" he pleaded. "Tell me why they would do this to you. Before you go running to the police. Give me a chance to correct things."

"Correct things? Look at my fucking face! Look at my back!" She winced as she pulled up her shirt so he could see her bruised shoulder where Grace had taken a bat to it. "They tried to kill me and all you care about is them. Once again! I don't even know why I'm surprised."

"I know this is bad but they're kids. They would never try anything like this unless they felt they had a good reason."

"So now it's my fault? Have you forgotten that I'm the victim?"

"I'm not saying that." He paused. "I admit, they did go too far but throwing them in jail is too much. They lost their mother last year, Roxanne. Don't make them lose their father and their freedom too."

"Like I said, all you care about is them," she yelled. "All you've ever cared about was them. My world is coming to an end and yet you sit over there and beg me to keep them safe. Who is going to keep me safe? Because it damn sure ain't you!"

Hollis was exhausted talking to her. She was going to do what she wanted and the only thing he could do was throw money on an attorney. Whatever she decided, he knew for a fact that he was done talking to her and he was done with the marriage also. "I should've never let you into my home. I should've known that a woman as young and as beautiful as you had other motives. So tell me, Roxanne, what are they? What did you really want with my family?"

Before she could answer, there was a loud crashing noise at the front door. "It's the police! Come out with your hands up!"

"What the fuck?" he yelled.

When the bedroom door came crashing down, Roxanne jumped against the headboard as she provided room for the policemen to get to Hollis. Five officers tackled Hollis to the floor and a pair of handcuffs was slapped around his wrists. He was roughly pulled up onto his feet. "Hollis Collins, you are under arrest for drug trafficking."

Hollis was whisked out of the house without another word. Now the girls were really alone.

For the next five days Roxanne ignored the girls. She left them to their sniffles and cries as they moaned about the loss of their father to the penitentiary. It turned out that all along Hollis was not employed by a candy factory like he claimed. Instead, he was a drug lord with a large operation that spanned the entire east coast. They had been building a case for years and after all of their hard work they finally got the boss. Mr. Hollis Collins himself.

The thread that led them to him came in a dumb way. When one of Hollis's trusted men called him on a phone that was supposed to be thrown away thirty days prior because it was also used to make drug sales, they caught on. Days later, they raided the spot dressed as a candy factory and found the barrels of sugar brought into the business were actually barrels of coke.

The Collins sisters were in Morgan's room wondering what would happen to them with their father gone when Roxanne entered holding a large brown paper bag. She sat it on the floor and clasped her fingers together in front of her.

Clearing her throat, she said, "As you know, your father has been arrested. But what you don't know is that your father may be getting twenty years for drug trafficking."

"My daddy ain't no dealer!" Grace yelled.

"Yeah, he's a manager at a candy factory," Lexia added.

Morgan remained silent because it was always obvious to her that something was up with their father. She figured he was a dealer a long time ago but after years of not being caught, she started to think she was wrong. Now, unfortunately, she learned she was right.

Unlike Morgan, the other sisters gasped and hugged one another in the middle of Morgan's floor when they heard the news. Up until that moment, they held on to hope that Hollis would be returning home soon. Now they didn't know if they would ever see him again, or if he would ever come home.

"Sweetheart, your father is a drug dealer. And since he's gone, I am in charge and things will be done differently around here," Roxanne picked up the bag and handed them all new diaries that had ugly metal witches on the front with long, sharp chins. It was the most hideous thing they'd ever seen in their lives. "Give me the other ones you've been writing in."

Morgan stood up, preparing to defend her sisters. "Roxanne, those are our personal—"

Her statement was cut short when Roxanne smacked her in the face. She rubbed her hand. "You have no idea how long I've been waiting to do that."

Grace jumped up, preparing to fight her again when she pulled out a gun and aimed at her, stopping her in place.

"Everybody stay where you are," Morgan begged them. She stood in front of her family. "Please." She looked at Roxanne. "Please don't hurt my sisters."

"I'm going to do just that if she touches me this time." She focused on Grace. "Do you hear me, bitch? I will shoot you dead and there won't be a jury in the world to convict me. Especially since I recorded my last scars." She looked at all of them one by one. "Now put the old diaries in the bag before I lose my patience." She pointed at it with the barrel of the gun.

All of the sisters walked to their rooms and returned with the diaries before dropping them in the bag. When Roxanne had all of them, she grinned. "Don't look so sad. I bought you new diaries because your lives as you knew them are changing and you'll need them to record new memories. With me, that is."

"What does that mean, Roxanne?" Morgan asked.

"It means what's getting ready to happen will be the worst time of your lives and I want to read every moment of it personally." She laughed as she backed out of the room, aiming at them until she closed the door.

Roxanne wasted no time stripping the Collins sisters of everything they loved. First, she took their diaries, and then she took their rooms, forcing them to all sleep in one room with Morgan. When they had nothing else, she took their freedom. They were not allowed in any other place of the house. Each night they would hear strangers in their home as Roxanne hosted parties in celebration of her new lifestyle. They even heard her making love to another man in their father's bedroom.

When Morgan asked her about it she took away all of their clothing and when school started she made an announcement that they would all be homeschooled by her. Of course she didn't teach them anything. She could care less if they were educated. In the end, all Roxanne did was put the sisters in total destitution.

And that wasn't the end of her cruel plan. Three weeks later, Morgan awoke to loud banging. She nudged Petra who was lying beside her on the bed. "Get up." She rubbed her eyes and leaned forward as if she could see what the sound was. "You hear that, Petra?"

Petra slowly sat up and rubbed her eyes. She sat on the edge of her bed and accidently placed her feet on Grace who was lying on the floor with Shaye and Lexia.

"Yeah." She stood up and stepped over her sisters. Slowly she walked toward the window. She looked out of it and peered down into the backyard. When she saw some men holding large slabs of wood, her eyes widened. "What is going on down there?" Before anybody could answer, a brown piece of wood was placed over the window blocking their view.

"Cut the light on, Petra," Morgan said.

Since the room was totally dark, Petra bumped around until she located the light switch. She flipped it on and Morgan jumped up and headed to the window. All she saw was wood and her heart thumped around. "What the fuck is she doing?" Morgan rushed toward the door and twisted the knob. It was locked. Normally she would leave it open for them to go to the bathroom but now they couldn't even go there.

Slowly Morgan turned around and observed her sisters. They were huddled in the middle of the floor.

"What's going on?" Grace asked hugging Lexia.

"She's turned the house into a coffin." Morgan said in a hushed tone. "I think she's going to bury us alive."

It had been three days since Roxanne added the wood panels and they had not seen her since. To use the bathroom they took turns peeing in a Big Gulp cup from 7-Eleven and when they had to shit they would do it in a trashcan in Morgan's closet. Since they hadn't eaten or drank anything, their mouths were pasty and they could feel death setting in on them. Morgan knew that if they didn't come up with a plan that they would die and she could not see that happening.

"We are going to have to kill her," Morgan said softly as she looked at the gaunt faces of her sisters. "It's her or us."

Petra nodded. "I've been waiting for you to say those words."

"So what's the plan?" Lexia asked.

"At some point she's going to come into this room." Morgan said as she walked closer to them. "I'm sure she has boarded up all of the windows and the doors downstairs too."

"How do we know she won't just leave us in here to die?" Grace asked.

"She will. I'm sure she will eventually. But first she'll want to see the looks on our faces when we see the house is boarded. She'll want to see the fright in our eyes. So I'm thinking she'll probably feed us a few more times. Trust me, this evil bitch gets off on this."

"So when she comes in the room, what do we do?" Grace asked.

"We yank her in here and finish what ya'll started in the basement. Except this time we won't let up until her heart stops beating."

So the Collins sisters waited. They waited two more days until they heard keys jingling at the door. It was midnight when the doorknob finally twisted and Morgan hopped up and nudged her sisters. "Wake up," she whispered. "She's coming in."

Since they already went through the plan, they were ready. Although they were weak, they knew this was their only moment if they were going to survive. The moment Roxanne opened the door, just as planned, Morgan yanked her inside by her hair, bringing her to her knees. Together they pounded her until she was flat and motionless on the floor.

When she stopped moving they all stood over her limp body. Grace walked closer and looked at Roxanne's closed eyes. "You think she's dead?"

Morgan walked closer to Roxanne. "Yes. I'm sure. I hit her as hard as I could." She moved toward the water pitcher and the sandwiches on the tray Roxanne was bringing in before she was bombarded. "Here, eat these."

The sisters clawed at the dry peanut butter sandwiches and washed them down with water. Roxanne's body lay at their feet like a carpet. They could care less about her life.

"Let me see if we can get out," Grace said before she ran through the house. When she came back she said, "All of the doors are locked. And the windows are covered too. Just like you said."

Morgan looked down at her body. "The key is probably on her. Inside of her jean pocket or something." She exhaled and looked at her closed eyes. "I gotta get it." The moment she bent down Roxanne pulled her by the wrist, bringing her to the floor. She slid a gun that was under her shirt from her waist and put it against Morgan's temple.

"Here I was being nice and you bitches tried to kill me again?" She cocked the gun and pressed it harder against Morgan's head.

"Please don't," Petra cried. "I'm begging you."

"Whoa," Roxanne snorted. "Since when have you begged for anybody? You're the selfish one, remember?"

"Now," she said as tears rolled down her face. "If you're going to kill us please give us our sister. Let us die together. I'm begging you."

Roxanne pushed Morgan toward the sisters and they all hugged her. She did it not because of sympathy but because killing her now would be too easy. She wanted Morgan to see her sisters suffer. "You all are going to pay for what you did to me. I promise." She rushed out of the door.

For two more days, the girls went without food and water again when suddenly the door opened and a tray full of bologna sandwiches with water was pushed inside of the room. This time Roxanne didn't bother to come empty-handed. She had a gun pointed at them with a bullet in the chamber.

When she closed the door the Collins sisters dug into the food without a second thought. Well, everyone but Petra who only drank the water after seeing it was not cloudy. Their hunger made the other sisters susceptible to being poisoned and she begged them not to eat the food. The only one who listened was Morgan.

Not even twelve hours later, everyone but Morgan and Petra became violently ill. And things got worse when one day Morgan woke up and Grace was missing. Weak from not having eaten, Morgan rolled out of bed and walked over to Lexia. She was sleeping on the floor and white froth spilled from the corners of her mouth. She, like the others, was dying. "Lexia, get up," Morgan was beside herself with anger for what Roxanne did to her sisters.

Lexia slowly opened her eyes. "What?"

"Grace is gone," she said frantically. "Did you see where she went?"

"No," she wailed. "I've been lying down."

Morgan asked Shaye and Petra and neither could recall anyone coming in the middle of the night and taking her. But that wouldn't stop the others from disappearing too. Roxanne would give them the water and food spiked with sleeping medicine and poison. And when they were out cold, she would take another Collins sister until the only ones left were Petra and Morgan.

When Petra woke up one morning and discovered that Morgan was so ill that she could not get out of bed, she decided that she would not go to sleep and allow her sister to die or be stolen in the night. She would wait up for Roxanne and refrain from drinking anything that would put her out. Although weak, she would use all of the energy she could spare to fight Roxanne again.

As always, Roxanne crept in the room at 3:00am with a tray of water and dry peanut butter sandwiches. But the moment she opened the door to push the food inside, Petra, who was standing behind the door, hit her over the head with Morgan's bat. Roxanne stumbled into the room and when she tried to reach for the gun in her shirt, Petra fought to wrestle it away from her.

Waking up in a daze, Morgan saw the struggle through blurry eyes and slowly got up to help. She didn't have a lot of energy but Morgan managed to get to the diary on the floor. She pulled off the witch's face and using the jagged chin, she jabbed it in Roxanne's throat until blood poured down her neck. When she was done she plopped to the floor out of exhaustion.

Roxanne finally stopped fighting and writhed on the floor, holding her neck. She pulled the witch out and tossed it to the floor. Blood oozed between her fingers and her eyes widened. They successfully overtook her.

"What did you do to me?" she whispered.

Petra picked up the gun and aimed it at her. "I saved my own life," Petra said standing over top of her head. "And the life of my sister."

Petra rushed toward Morgan and helped her up. "Come on, we gotta get out of here."

"No," Morgan moaned. "I can barely move like this." She didn't have enough energy to get up, let alone run.

"We gotta go," Petra demanded as she helped her to her feet.

Slowly the two of them limped out of the room, leaving Roxanne alone to choke on her own blood. Petra closed and locked the door and took Morgan to her father's room. For a week she nursed her until she was back to good health.

One Monday morning, Morgan rolled over, as Petra was coming in. "We have to find our sisters," she said as a tear rolled down her face. Since she was getting better, the realization of their life finally hit her. "Unless...I mean...do you think she killed them?"

Petra sat on the edge of the bed and handed her a red leather book. "What's this?" Morgan asked as she sat up and leaned against the headboard.

"This is where our sisters are."

Morgan's eyes widened. "They aren't..." She choked up.

"Nope. She sold them." Petra took the book from her and opened it up. "Look, there are the names of the people and next to their names are prices."

Morgan took the book back as her eyes rolled over the pages. "What the fuck was wrong with that bitch?"

"She sold them into prostitution. And we have to bring them back." She paused. "At least we know where they are."

Morgan nodded slowly. Part of her was relieved that they were alive and the other part was devastated that they had to go through this. First they lost their mother, then their father and now they were separated from the only family they had left. Their sisters.

Morgan and Petra packed their clothes and their most important items. Before leaving, Morgan opened her father's secret safe and pulled out a few stacks of money that the cops didn't seize in the arrest.

As they walked down the steps to the front door, Petra asked, "What do you think we should do about the body?"

"Nothing. What do we care?"

"But we'll be on the run forever," Petra persisted.

"We gonna be on the run anyway, Petra. I'm eighteen now but you guys are still underage. The only way we can stay together is if it's illegal." Morgan put a hand on her shoulder. "Let's go."

They walked out of the door and toward Morgan's car. They loaded the bags in the trunk and Morgan climbed into the driver's seat. Petra walked to the passenger side and said, "Oh, I forgot something else inside. Give me one minute, sis."

"Want me to go with you?"

"No." She smiled. "It won't be but a second."

Petra walked back into the house and closed the door. She was inside for five minutes before she rushed back outside and jumped in the car. "Pull off! Quick!" Petra yelled looking at the house.

Morgan was scared. "What did you do?"

"Just leave!"

"Answer the question!" Morgan demanded, slapping the steering wheel.

Petra swallowed and looked at the house again. Morgan followed her gaze and she could see smoke billowing from the window.

"You didn't," Morgan said.

"Only fire can cleanse it now so let it burn."

THE MEANEST OF THEM ALL

The Cartel Collection
Established in January 2008
We're growing stronger by the month!!!
www.thecartelpublications.com

Cartel Publications Order Form
Inmates <u>ONLY</u> get novels for $10.00 per book!

Titles	_Fee_
Shyt List	$15.00
Shyt List 2	$15.00
Pitbulls In A Skirt	$15.00
Pitbulls In A Skirt 2	$15.00
Pitbulls In A Skirt 3	$15.00
Pitbulls In A Skirt 4	$15.00
Victoria's Secret	$15.00
Poison	$15.00
Poison 2	$15.00
Hell Razor Honeys	$15.00
Hell Razor Honeys 2	$15.00
A Hustler's Son 2	$15.00
Black And Ugly As Ever	$15.00
Year of The Crack Mom	$15.00
The Face That Launched a Thousand Bullets	$15.00
The Unusual Suspects	$15.00
Miss Wayne & The Queens of DC	$15.00
Year of The Crack Mom	$15.00
Paid in Blood	$15.00
Shyt List III	$15.00
Shyt List IV	$15.00
Raunchy	$15.00
Raunchy 2	$15.00
Raunchy 3	$15.00
Jealous Hearted	$15.00
Quita's Dayscare Center	$15.00
Quita's Dayscare Center 2	$15.00
Shyt List V	$15.00
Deadheads	$15.00
Pretty Kings	$15.00
Pretty Kings II	$15.00
Drunk & Hot Girls	$15.00
Hersband Material	$15.00
Upscale Kittens	$15.00
Wake & Bake Boys	$15.00
Young & Dumb	$15.00
Tranny 911	$15.00
Tranny 911: Dixie's Rise	$15.00
First Comes Love Then Comes Murder	$15.00
Young & Dumb: Vyce's Getback	$15.00
Luxury Tax	$15.00
Mad Maxxx	$15.00
The Lying King	$15.00
Crazy Kind of Love	$15.00
Silence of the Nine	$15.00
Prison Throne	$15.00
The Pussy Mob	$15.00
The Meanest of Them All	$15.00

Please add $4.00 per book for shipping and handling.
The Cartel Publications * P.O. Box 486 * Owings Mills * MD * 21117

Name: _____

Address:_____

City/State:_____

Contact # & Email:_____

*Please allow 5-7 business days for delivery. The Cartel is not
responsible for prison orders rejected.*

Personal Checks Are Not Accepted.

The Pussy MOB

A NOVEL BY

CHANEL MURPHY

GOON

T. STYLES

NATIONAL BEST SELLING AUTHOR OF *RAUNCHY*

Only copy - 2018

Made in the USA
Lexington, KY
03 July 2014